An Ezra Melamed Mystery

the Disappearing Dowry

Libi Astaire

A Zahav Press Book

First published 2009
Copyright © 2009 by Zahav Press
ISBN 978-1-56871-501-8

Published and distributed by:
Zahav Press
5809 16th Avenue
Brooklyn, NY 11204
E-mail: info@zahavpress.com
www.zahavpress.com

Prologue

Written by the Work's Author

ALL BEGINNINGS ARE HARD, AS our Sages inform us. And so even a thing which should be the simplest thing in the world — such as two young ladies of similar tastes and background becoming the best of friends — is fraught with obstacles and frustrations of the most extraordinary nature. This is especially true if both their families do not have seats in the Ladies' Section of our Great Synagogue — which is located at Duke's Place in the City of London, as everyone in England knows, after the royal visit last year by three sons of His Majesty King George III, namely the Royal Dukes of Cambridge, Cumberland, and Essex, and other persons of the titled class.

In this unhappy circumstance, the two young ladies must meet by chance at a suitably chaperoned public venue, such as the grounds of London's Hyde Park, the Pump Room at Bath, or the Seaside Promenade at Brighton. Upon the first meeting they may exchange nods of the head. Upon the second, they may exchange a few innocuous words about the weather. The next step is for one of the young ladies to leave her visiting card at the residence of the other one. This will be followed by an invitation from the second young lady to take a morning walk with her and her mother and sisters, or perhaps a similarly chaperoned ride in her carriage — of course, this will be in a *closed* carriage, as we are speaking of two young ladies who come from respectable Jewish homes.

Should the friendship have proceeded thus far without mishap, the first young lady will invite her new friend for chocolate. The second will extend an invitation to dinner. And then — finally! — after dinner the two young ladies will seat themselves in a quiet corner in the drawing room and pour out their hearts and confide their most cherished secrets and dreams, as only two young ladies about to reach the "marriageable" age can do.

This long and drawn out protocol — as difficult to negotiate as the Peace of Amiens between England and France — may be very fine for some. However, I say as follows: You don't know me.

I don't know you. But why should that prevent us from becoming good friends from the very first moment of our acquaintance, which is now? Especially when I have the most extraordinary tale to tell you!

Ah, I know what you are thinking. She is a tale-bearer? I want nothing to do with a young lady like her!

But before you turn away, please give me a moment to explain. My tale is not one of slander or gossip. It is a tale written in the tradition of our people: a family *megillah*, or scroll, in which I will describe, as a most impartial Observer and with most exacting detail — along with certain excursions into the *picturesque*, which is so popular during our times, thanks to the novels of Mrs. Radcliffe, and others — the terrible ordeal that my family has recently endured, and how we were miraculously saved from most certain ruin by the One Above, may His Great Name be praised.

And should you wonder why the important task of chronicling my family's history has been given to a person as young and inconsequential as this Author, the reason is as follows: The hero of our story, Mr. Ezra Melamed — who was sent by Hashem to help us solve the great mystery (Hashem is the Name that we Jews commonly use for the Supreme Being that Englishmen refer to as G-d) — politely informed me that he is a collector of books, and not a writer of them. My older sister, Hannah, a principal character in this narrative, is happily far too busy to be bothered with such inky matters. My mother, Mrs. Rose Lyon, is similarly occupied with family concerns. And as for my father, Mr. Samuel Lyon, it is true that he has the skill and could perhaps spare a few hours from his busy day, which is partly spent at his fashionable clock-making shop and partly spent in learning Torah. However, when I broached the subject of who should write this family *megillah*, my father declined to be its Author. Glancing over at the two cabinets sitting in our drawing room, which are filled with examples of my paintings on china, he said to my mother, "Better that Rebecca should try her hand at writing a book than paint more china plates, for we have no room for another cabinet."

Thus, with the permission and blessings of all concerned, I begin my story.

Devonshire Square, London, England
Chanukah 5571/December 1810

Chapter One

"WHAT CAN BE TAKING THEM so long? It is so unlike your father to be so inconsiderate."

Mrs. Rose Lyon, an amiable wife, mother, and woman of valor, glanced over at the closed door. On the other side of that wooden encumbrance was the library, a room that normally did not hold much interest for the lady of the house. But on this particular evening the library was the center of the entire family's attention, for it was there that Mr. Samuel Lyon, the family patriarch, was engaged in conversation with Mr. Mayer Goldsmith.

"Papa and Mr. Goldsmith must have a great deal

to talk about," replied Hannah, the eldest daughter of the Lyon family. She did not raise her eyes from the white tablecloth she was embroidering, although the blush in her cheeks revealed to all that she, too, was more than a little interested in the conversation taking place in the next room.

"I disagree," said Mrs. Lyon. "You, my dear Hannah, are the finest eighteen-year-old girl in the world. Mr. Goldsmith's son, David, is the finest twenty-one-year-old boy in the world. What could be more natural than for the two of you to be married?"

"There are the financial matters to consider, Mama," said Hannah, still sewing and still blushing. "Perhaps Mr. Goldsmith is hoping to secure a greater fortune for his only son."

"Nonsense! Mr. Goldsmith may have recently sold half the contents of his jeweler's shop to the Duke of York, but everyone knows that Royal Dukes buy on credit and so it will be years before Mr. Goldsmith sees his money. Your father is the match of Mr. Goldsmith — or any Jewish merchant in London — when it comes to real wealth or, for that matter, a noble clientele."

Mrs. Lyon suddenly glanced nervously about the room. To boast of one's good fortune was to invite the Evil Eye to unleash its malicious powers. And so even though Mrs. Lyon prided herself upon being born and bred in London, the most modern and advanced city in Europe, she quickly called upon the powerful remedy against the Evil Eye that she had learned from her grandmother, who had learned it as a child from *her* grandmother in her native city of Prague.

"Pooh! Pooh! Pooh!" said Mrs. Lyon, in rapid succession and with quick determination. Then, just to make sure that her carelessly spoken words would do no harm, she uttered the following blessings, "May the Holy One, Blessed be His Name, bless all the Jews of England and elsewhere with prosperity, good health, and peace! And G-d save the King!"

"Amen, amen," replied her children.

Having thus disposed of the Evil Eye, Mrs. Lyon returned her attention to the matter at hand and called to her second eldest daughter, "Rebecca, do you not feel the need for some exercise?"

(Reader, this daughter called Rebecca is I! But I have already revealed to you my secret: For the purpose of the telling of this story, I have disguised myself behind the sphinx-like visage of the Narrator.)

Rebecca looked up from the china plate that she was painting with surprise. "Do you mean to take a walk around Devonshire Square at this late hour, Mama?"

"Of course not, Rebecca. But I thought we might take a few turns around the room."

As Mrs. Lyon had already stood up, Rebecca

had no choice but to set aside her paintbrush and dutifully comply. Mother and daughter walked together, arm in arm, down the length of the room. When they reached the end, Mrs. Lyon lingered for several moments, her head slightly tilted toward the closed door.

"Mama, put your ear to the keyhole! You'll hear ever so much better," advised Joshua, who at the tender age of five had shown himself more than once to be a master at overhearing private conversations.

"My precious child, I shall do nothing of the sort," said Mrs. Lyon sternly, as she reluctantly walked away from the door. "Nothing is further from my mind than to intrude upon a conversation that I have not been invited to participate in. And I am most surprised that a child of mine should advise such a course of action. If I did not know that you are small for your age and therefore unable to reach the keyhole, I do not know what I should think."

"But I can reach the keyhole," Joshua protested. Then he ran to fetch a footstool, which he carried over to the door. After carefully removing his slippers, so as not to leave a mark on the silk brocade fabric, he climbed upon the footstool and pressed his ear to the keyhole.

"Joshua! Get away from that door at once!" **Hannah cried out.**

"Hush, Hannah," Joshua replied. "How's a fellow to hear?"

"Your sister is right, Joshua," Mrs. Lyon said with a small sigh. After a few seconds had passed, she added, "Please put the footstool back in its place."

Joshua made a great show of climbing down from his perch and sticking his feet into his slippers. "Very well, Mama, if you insist."

"I hope you did not hear even three words, Joshua," said Mrs. Lyon, as she watched her son push the footstool back in its place.

"I didn't hear three, and I didn't hear two," Joshua replied with a mischievous smile. "But I did hear Papa and Mr. Goldsmith say one word."

"And what word was that?" asked Rebecca, since she knew that her mother and Hannah could hardly interrogate the little imp after chastising Joshua for his transgression.

"*L'chaim!*"

"What?" Mrs. Lyon exclaimed, as she looked from Joshua to Hannah and then over to the door, before collapsing onto a nearby chair and bursting into joyful tears.

Hannah, meanwhile, had let her piece of embroidery fall to the floor and risen from her chair. Rebecca rushed over to Hannah to shower her with kisses, while their two younger sisters, Esther and Sarah, joined hands and began to twirl around the floor.

The two younger Miss Lyons were just about to crash into Joshua, who was busy jumping up and down from excitement, when the door to the library swung open and Mr. Lyon and Mr. Goldsmith entered the room.

"*Mazel tov*, Mrs. Lyon!" Mr. Lyon cried out. "*Mazel tov*, Hannah! You're a..."

Mr. Lyon, noticing the scene taking place in his drawing room with more than a little dismay, fell silent.

"It appears, Lyon," Mr. Goldsmith said with a smile, "that your family has already heard the news."

Chapter Two

THE WEDDING WAS SET FOR three months hence, a few weeks before Rosh Hashanah, the Jewish New Year. At one moment Mrs. Lyon exclaimed that she didn't know how she could ever wait that long, for she was that excited. At the next, the happy mother of the bride fretted that she should never finish with all the preparations in time. At every moment, the entire household was turned completely upside down in the most joyous way.

The front door was continually being opened and closed, as one neighbor after another came to say *mazel tov* to Mrs. Lyon and fuss over Hannah.

The drawing room had turned into a tea room, or so it seemed, for Perl, their maid, was constantly refilling the family's best silver teapot and bringing up platters of freshly baked cake. But after the first excitement had died down and the family was having tea alone for the first time in more than a week, Mrs. Lyon's face assumed a very serious expression.

"Tomorrow, Hannah, dear, we must go to the dressmaker," she said. "I shall order a carriage for eleven o'clock. If there is time, we shall also go to the linen-draper. However, I am not optimistic."

Rebecca glanced over at Hannah and gave her sister a look of commiseration. Hannah returned this sisterly show of support with a wan smile.

In many ways the two sisters were very different. Hannah was everything a Daughter of Israel should be: She was even-tempered and kind-hearted; she was intelligent and orderly and capable; and despite her family's wealth, which would have entitled her to spend her days in leisure, she devoted several afternoons a week to a benevolent society for the Jewish community's orphaned children.

Rebecca, on the other hand, was quite impossible. When she wasn't fidgeting from impatience, she was reading the latest novel or staring out the window, lost in a world of her own. Her painting and embroidery supplies were scattered in every room of the house, so that she could never find the colors or brushes or scissors that she needed. Although she, too, was touched by the plight of others less fortunate, her plans to assist them were so grandiose that they could not be accomplished in their entirety, and so she would lose heart and accomplish nothing at all. And then she would be out of sorts for days.

However, the two sisters were alike in one way: They both hated to make a fuss about clothes. And in this they were their mother's despair.

"What is the point in having daughters, if a mother can't talk to them about bonnets and bows?" Mrs. Lyon was heard to say on more than one occasion.

"Whatever you choose for me will be fine," Hannah would say.

And poor Mrs. Lyon could say nothing in reply. She could hardly complain about having so dutiful a daughter!

Once the engagement had been announced, though, Hannah could no longer demur. She was now a *kallah*, a bride, and so she must have a new wardrobe that would reflect her new status in the community. The Goldsmiths would expect that of their prospective daughter-in-law, and the last thing Hannah wished to do was cause Mrs. Goldsmith anguish and embarrassment because she had been seen in public wearing last year's bonnet.

And so this is why Rebecca's heart went out

to her sister. Rebecca knew that the trip to the dressmaker was just the beginning. In that hallowed place, fashion sketches would be carefully studied and passionately discussed as though they were pages from the Talmud. It could take days for Mrs. Lyon to decide upon a pattern. Then she would take Hannah to the linen-drapers, to decide upon a fabric, and the whole agonizing process would begin anew. But still the ordeal would not be over, for who ever heard of a dress that did not have buttons or trim? And so the carriage would next be instructed to take poor Hannah to the haberdashers, where she would be required to wade through shimmering rivers of ribbons and lace and braid, and deep ponds of buttons and beads — all of which came in more colors than the uncluttered mind could imagine or a simple heart desire. And still the trial would not be over. When the fabric and trimmings were selected, it was back to the dressmaker for a first, second, perhaps even third fitting.

And that was just the dress.

Next in importance came the bonnet and hat, for no respectable woman — even a married Jewish woman who covered her hair with a wig — would so much as step outside her door without something on her head. It wouldn't do for Hannah to tell Mrs. Lyon that she could spruce up her old bonnet with a bit of colored ribbon. Since ladies' fashions were as changeable as the rates on the

Stock Exchange — and since the wrong headgear could ruin the effect of even the most exquisitely designed dress — the trip to the milliner was a most serious and necessary business.

But a dress and bonnet did not a complete outfit make. Short Spencer jackets and long pelisses must also be ordered from the dressmaker; hose and stockings must be bought at the hosier; shoes, boots, and slippers at the shoemaker; gloves, parasols, and reticules at the makers of gloves, umbrellas, and purses; and a hundred other little things bought at a hundred other little shops and stalls.

And that was just for Hannah. Presents must be bought for the bridegroom. A house must be found for the young couple, and furnished.

Rebecca could feel her head start to swim. She was feeling wonderfully thankful that she was still young enough to be spared all these torments. While Hannah was being dragged all about London, she would be able to stay in their comfortable home in Devonshire Square and quietly paint her china plates.

Then her mother interrupted her thoughts and said, "And you, Rebecca, shall come with us. You have such a good eye for color, I am sure your assistance shall prove to be invaluable."

❖ ❖ ❖

AS WAS MENTIONED IN THE Prologue to this work, a *megillah* is not a *megillah* if it does not offer words of thanksgiving and praise to the One Who works miracles for His people, great and small. And so here the Author must perform her duty and proclaim: Thank You, Hashem, for Your many kindnesses! Not only did the first dressmaker visited have an illustrated ladies' fashion magazine with all the latest sketches from France, but there was even a bridal gown that found favor in Mrs. Lyon's eyes! Hannah also smiled when she saw it, for it truly was the prettiest dress that could be imagined.

"The garment is constructed from white satin, and so it is perfectly modest," the dressmaker explained. "The deep flounce at the bottom is trimmed with Brussels lace. I can recommend a haberdasher who carries just the thing."

The dressmaker did not even bother to lower her voice, even though it should have been impossible for an English tradesman to procure any goods from the European Continent. This was due to the economic blockade against England imposed by Napoleon. However, everyone knew that a whole corps of smugglers, sanctioned by the English government, was doing a brisk business of smuggling English goods to the Continent and bringing back to English markets many of the necessary things in life, such as fine wines and fashion illustrations from France and delicate laces from Belgium.

"And the tight wreath of roses above the flounce? Must the flowers be made of white satin, or could a pale rose color do as well?" asked Mrs. Lyon, still pensively studying the sketch.

"In France, the young ladies of quality prefer the simplicity of a pure white rose," replied the dressmaker, with an air of authority.

That settled it. Wellington and Napoleon might be battling it out in Portugal and Spain, but the fashionable ladies of England had no quarrel with their elegant counterparts in France, who were universally acknowledged for their superior taste. With a copy of the fashion illustration firmly clasped in her hand, Mrs. Lyon ordered the carriage to proceed to the linen-draper's shop. After much deliberation, a decision concerning the satin fabric was finally made. Then Mrs. Lyon and her two daughters gratefully climbed into the waiting carriage, which transported the weary party to their home. They had accomplished a great deal, Mrs. Lyon commented with satisfaction. "But tomorrow I hope we shall accomplish a great deal more."

Chapter Three

EACH EVENING AT DINNERTIME, MRS. Lyon informed Mr. Lyon of all the purchases she had made that day, describing the encounter in each shop with the most precise detail. He listened with an amused expression on his face, sometimes congratulating Mrs. Lyon for keeping the English economy afloat during wartime, sometimes feigning shock that a little thing like a reticule, which barely held more than a lady's comb and handkerchief, could cost so much. Always he concluded the day's narrative by turning to Hannah and saying, "As long as you are happy, my dear."

However, when he retired to his library and

glanced through the tradesmen's bills piled high upon his desk, his face showed concern and not amusement. Rebecca knew this, for one evening she had entered the library to retrieve a book, and she was surprised to see her father with such an unusual expression.

"Is something wrong, Papa?" she asked.

Mr. Lyon pushed aside the bills and smiled. "On the contrary. This is a happy time for all of us. I am only a little surprised by how much it costs to turn a perfectly charming young lady like your sister into a respectable married woman. From these bills, someone might mistakenly think that I have deprived my daughter of shoes and parasols all her life and now must rush to make amends."

"Yet it is a good thing that young people get married, is it not? You have given trade to the owners of the dressmaker and milliner shops, but other fathers come to your shop and buy longcase clocks for their children's new homes. Surely, their money will pay your bills, just as your money will pay theirs."

"You have perfectly described the world of economics in its simplest and purest form, Rebecca. And if this were the way of the world, perhaps we might have less but we would be better off. However, this is not the way of the world, for you have left out one highly important element from your equation: Credit."

"No, Papa, I have not. No tradesman would expect someone like Mama to enter his shop clutching a pouch filled with heavy coins in her hand. It is assumed that after she has made her selection, the bill will be sent round to her home and that payment will be made at a later time."

"And if it is not?"

Rebecca gave her father a puzzled look.

"In our circles, Rebecca, we are careful to pay off our debts in a timely manner. We have the Torah to guide us in all things, including our business activities. However, there are people who live by different laws."

"The Royal Dukes?"

"And others, too. They pay their debts to tradesmen when they please, and sometimes not at all. They can do this because, unlike ordinary people who cannot pay their bills, an English nobleman cannot be thrown into debtors' prison."

Rebecca's face turned pale. "Oh, Papa!" she exclaimed. "Shall we go to gaol then, because of all our purchases?"

"Not at all," Mr. Lyon replied with a laugh. "I tell you this not to alarm you, my child, but to warn you. Some day you will be married, with Hashem's help. It will be your responsibility to manage your family's household. If you buy only what you can afford to pay for, you will not be sorry. But that's enough of economics for one night."

"May I ask one more question?"

"If the question concerns a carriage that a certain young lady wishes her father would purchase, the answer is no."

Rebecca tried not to smile. Ever since her good friend Harriet Franks, who had moved to Mayfair the previous year, returned to Devonshire Square for visits in her family's newly purchased landau, Rebecca had dreamt of owning a carriage, too. The Franks's landau was a roomy carriage that was pulled by four beautiful chestnut horses. The carriage had a soft folding top that was divided into two sections, so that one or both sides could be let down on fine days. Mr. Lyon did not approve of young ladies driving through London in an open — even a half-open — carriage. But even when both sides of the hood were pulled up and latched tight, the carriage was still a handsome sight. To her great disappointment, though, Mr. Lyon had dismissed the idea of owning a carriage as being woefully extravagant. However, this was not Rebecca's question.

"I was wondering, Papa, if the nobility don't pay their bills, why do you sell to them?"

Mr. Lyon smiled. "There's many a tradesman in London who has the same question," he replied. "But what can we do? One merchant cannot refuse to sell to them, for if he did he should be ostracized by all of society. And the gentry do perform a valuable service, even when they don't pay their bills. When a duke or an earl decides that he must have a longcase clock from Mr. Lyon, clockmaker, the bankers and well-to-do merchants follow his lead. Suddenly, no fashionable home can be without one."

"Do the bankers and well-to-do merchants pay their bills?"

"Yes, Rebecca, on the whole they do. But I do not wish to mislead you. There are many fine earls and lords who are scrupulous in this matter, as well. We mustn't let the questionable behavior of a few gentlemen lower our regard for the whole of society."

Thus reassured, Rebecca selected her book and returned to the drawing room, where she spent a happy evening wandering through the picturesque scenes of Jerusalem and the Holy Land, as depicted by an author and illustrator who had been there. If from time to time a landau drawn by two pairs of perfectly matched chestnut horses stole into the Biblical scene, it was no fault of the book's illustrator. Rather, the fault belonged to the reader, whose imagination, unlike the horses, had not yet been sufficiently trained.

And so the days and evenings passed. Everyone was so busy preparing for the wedding that no one thought to complain that the family would not be going to Brighton that year, as was their custom, to escape the heat of the city and enjoy the healthful sea air. However, the decision to remain in London all summer was not because Mr. Lyon was busy with finding a suitable home for the young couple and Mrs. Lyon was busy with furnishing it.

Not long after Mr. Lyon informed the proprietor of Baer's Coffee House — a respectable coffee house owned by Mr. Lyon's good friend, Mr. Asher Baer — that he was looking to rent an apartment suitable for a young couple, he was informed that the upper two floors of a fine house on nearby Bury Street were available. Since the house in question was owned by a mutual acquaintance and fellow member of the Great Synagogue's congregation, a Mr. Ezra Melamed, the details of the rental agreement were quickly and amicably settled over a cup of Mr. Baer's excellent brew.

To Mr. Lyon's considerable relief, and Mrs. Lyon's just as considerable chagrin, the two floors came furnished with everything a young couple could possibly need. This was so because the rooms had been outfitted for Mr. Melamed's youngest daughter and her husband, and Mr. Melamed — who came from one of the more established Jewish families in London and was known for both his great wealth and his good taste — had spared no expense. However, the newly married couple unexpectedly departed for New York not long after they moved in, and so the rooms became unexpectedly available just when Mr. Lyon needed them for his own daughter.

Deprived of this motherly pleasure of choosing wallpapers and carpets for Hannah's first home, Mrs. Lyon might have drowned her disappointment in the invigorating seawaters of Brighton except for another interesting complication, namely, the bridegroom.

After the terms of the engagement had been formalized, it was the community's custom that the young woman and the young man should not meet again until the wedding. Since Miss Lyon lived at one end of Devonshire Square and Mr. Goldsmith lived at the other end, there was no way to prevent an accidental meeting except by locking up the young people in their respective chambers. Although locking up young people in dark and deserted towers once happened with alarming frequency in Italy — if the very popular novels of Mrs. Radcliffe are to be believed — this was England, and in England such things aren't done. Therefore, another remedy had to be devised.

If the Emperor Napoleon would have been more obliging, it might have been possible to send Mr. David Goldsmith to the Continent for several months, to learn Torah in one of the famed *yeshivos* that are the pride of European Jewry. But times being what they were, such a plan was fraught with danger. Even if a letter of safe passage was somehow procured, there was no guarantee that the French would honor it. There were reports that some English travelers had been thrown into gaol, and so Mr. Lyon could not fault Mr. Goldsmith for not wishing to take such a risk with the life of his only son.

And so it was decided that the most practical solution was for the Goldsmith family to go to Brighton, while the Lyon family would remain in London.

"Mr. Goldsmith always closes his shop after the London season has ended," Mr. Lyon explained to his family. "He follows the gentry to Brighton, where he also has a shop. I imagine that David will assist his father there, as he does here in town, for I've heard that the sea air is very good for a jeweler's business. It gives certain people a tremendous appetite for trinkets made of diamonds and pearls."

Mrs. Lyon coughed, which was her way of signaling to Mr. Lyon that enough had been said. The topic of Brighton was dropped, and the conversation turned to another one.

Hannah had said nothing during the conversation about Brighton, and Rebecca was much surprised to see that her sister took the news so calmly. Although she had no doubt that the young Mr. Goldsmith intended to conduct himself with absolute propriety, Rebecca was equally sure that Brighton in the summertime was more dangerous for a rich and handsome young man (and Mr. David Goldsmith was both) than the most deserted, banditti-infested mountain pass found in any Gothic novel. There were separate bathing areas in Brighton for the ladies and the gentlemen, of course. However, the resort's famous Promenade was an entirely different story. There eligible young ladies, decked out in all their finery, were more plentiful than seashells. It would be impossible to avoid them, no matter how hard a young Mr. Goldsmith might try. And what if one of these young ladies should try to win his heart? Poor Hannah would know nothing about it until it was too late.

However, when Rebecca expressed her fears to Hannah, after the two sisters had retired to their room for the night, Hannah absolutely refused to give credence to them. "He will not be in Brighton alone," she reminded Rebecca, "and he will be much too busy in the shop to take afternoon walks."

The discussion was seemingly closed. If neither Hannah nor their parents were concerned, then surely there was nothing for Rebecca to be worried about. That night, however, Rebecca awoke from her troubled sleep with a start. If she had been stolen away from her comfortable bed by agents from the Inquisition and thrown into a piteously dark and narrow cell — as happened to the hero of

The Italian, a very popular novel by Mrs. Radcliffe — she was sure that she could not have been more terrified. The voice of reason could not calm her. The demands of faith and trust in the One Who guides the world could not comfort her. She knew that something terrible was about to happen.

And she was right.

Chapter Four

THE TERROR THAT REBECCA ANTICIPATED did not manifest itself immediately. The sun continued to rise as usual and cast its cheerful glow upon the slowly awakening city of London. Horses plodded down the cobblestone streets, dragging behind them wagons filled with colorful vegetables from the countryside, live chickens and fresh eggs, and whatever other produce the farmers had to sell. And every morning the fruit sellers and fishmongers drowsily made their way to their market squares and readied their stalls for another day of haggling and selling.

One morning, though, an unusual occurrence

did happen in that teeming, bustling metropolis. Rebecca Lyon, who usually had to be pulled out from underneath her bedcovers in the morning, sprang from her bed even before the maid came to wake her, and she was already dressed and standing at the sitting room's window, which overlooked the square, when the others came down for breakfast. The source of this newly found wellspring of alacrity was easily discovered. This was the morning that the Goldsmith family was to set off for Brighton.

"The coachmen are handing up the luggage now," she informed the others, who were decorously seated around the breakfast table. "There's Mrs. Goldsmith! She does look elegant in her traveling costume. She's wearing a pale peach pelisse trimmed with a pomona green braid."

Although Rebecca was much more interested in the carriage — which was a coach-and-four — she knew her mother would be interested in what Mrs. Goldsmith was wearing.

"Pale peach? To travel in?" murmured Mrs. Lyon, a hint of disapproval in her voice. "How ever will she keep it clean? There's so much dust on these roads, I fear her outfit shall be ruined."

"Perhaps she doesn't care if she ruins it," Rebecca replied. "The Goldsmiths are rich. She can buy a new traveling outfit in Brighton."

"That would be intentionally wasteful," said Mr.

Lyon. "If you must stand at the window, Rebecca, please do us the favor of judging the actions of the Goldsmiths favorably."

"Papa is right," said Hannah. "A carriage becomes very stuffy on a hot day. Perhaps the peach pelisse is the most comfortable coat in Mrs. Goldsmith's wardrobe."

Mr. Lyon nodded his head in approval and returned to his morning newspaper, while Rebecca returned her attention to the goings-on in the square. Mr. Goldsmith and David Goldsmith were speaking to one of the coachmen, while a servant helped Mrs. Goldsmith into the carriage. The crucial moment was approaching, and Rebecca focused all of her attention upon the young man.

She had always liked David Goldsmith, for what was there not to like? He was friendly without being frivolous or overbearing; he could read the Torah portion in Hebrew — which he chanted in a pleasant voice when he was called upon to do so on Shabbos mornings in their synagogue — and he could decipher a page of the Talmud, but he never boasted about his learning; and although he was blessed with a handsome appearance, he didn't succumb to the dandyism which was so prevalent during those days.

Yet even while Rebecca noted with approval his dark blue morning coat and sensibly tied cravat, she was not staring at the young man so intently because she was interested in his clothes. Everyone knew that the hero of a story couldn't just get into a carriage and drive away, leaving behind his betrothed without a glance or a sigh. And so she was very curious to see how the young Mr. Goldsmith would express his distress at being parted from Hannah for the next few months.

"Rebecca, your breakfast is getting cold," Mrs. Lyon called out.

Rebecca refused to be torn from her post at the window, even though her stomach was starting to rumble. And she was presently rewarded for her steadfastness. The elder Mr. Goldsmith finished his conversation with the coachman and climbed into the carriage. David Goldsmith, who had been holding open the carriage door for his father, suddenly lifted his head and looked in the direction of the Lyon family's home. For several seconds he gazed up at the sitting room's empty window (it was empty because Rebecca had dashed behind the gauzy curtain, through which she could see but not be seen) with a wistful expression on his face. Then someone inside the carriage must have called to him, because he turned his head away from the window and got into the carriage.

The carriage door was closed. The coachmen took their places. And then it was over. The coach had left the square and the Goldsmith family was **on their way to Brighton.**

Rebecca turned away from the window with her sentiments satisfied. A sharp pang of hunger reminded her that the time had come to perform a similar service for her empty stomach, and so she took her place at the table, where a delicious breakfast was waiting for her.

❖ ❖ ❖

MR. LYON LISTENED FROM THE back room of his shop as his new assistant, Isaac Warburg, a recent arrival to England from Germany, explained to a customer the advantages of an eight-day longcase clock over the significantly cheaper thirty-hour clock. He made a note that the young man slightly mispronounced the word *pendulum*. They would have to work on that after the customer left. But all in all the young man was doing a fine job, which was a relief.

It hadn't been easy finding a replacement for his former assistant, Jacob Oppenheim, who had moved to Manchester to set up his own shop. Mr. Lyon was happy that Jacob Oppenheim was ambitious, and he wished the young man well, but he dearly felt the absence of such an able assistant. Being an assistant in Mr. Lyon's shop required a good knowledge of both cabinet-making and clock-making, since the design and manufacture of longcase clocks was a substantial part of Mr. Lyon's business. The assistant also had to be polished enough in his speech and appearance to wait upon the wealthy customers who visited the shop.

Although Mr. Lyon had not moved his business to the very fashionable Mayfair district, as some of the other Jewish merchants were starting to do, his location on Cornhill Street was still considered to be a good one. Cornhill's close proximity to the triumvirate of English finance — the Bank of England, the Royal Exchange, and the Stock Exchange — ensured that the street's clockmakers, jewelers, print shops, and coffee houses did a brisk business, and so the assistant had to know how to handle the stockbroker or merchant who had recently made a fortune on the 'Xchange. Mr. Lyon, of course, dealt personally with the earls and lords, usually going to their townhouses to spare them the trouble of traveling to the East End.

Yet there was another reason why Mr. Lyon missed his former assistant. It had been their habit to set aside one hour a day to learn Talmud, and this had been the highlight of Mr. Lyon's day. Since Jacob Oppenheim had a sharp mind, it had been a pleasure to sit together over the large tome and try to unravel the intricate arguments of the great Talmudic Sages. He might have considered the young man as a suitable match for Hannah, except that Mr. Oppenheim had no fortune. The young immigrant from Bohemia had arrived in England a few years earlier with little more than the clothes on his back — due to a trumped-up charge of dealing in contraband that was brought against him and which had necessitated his hasty flight from his place of birth — and his only money was what he had set aside while working in Mr. Lyon's shop.

Mr. Lyon felt a special obligation to help out these new immigrants in whatever limited way he could. Whereas the average Englishman only had to contend with the French, English Jews had a whole host of problems on the Continent to deal with. Repressive restrictions in Germany, Bohemia, and Poland had resulted in the emigration of thousands of Jews, who were streaming into London with the hope of making their fortune in England's more tolerant social climate. However, only a few of them were like Jacob Oppenheim and Isaac Warburg, young men who had grown up in good homes and received a good education and so were easily employable. The vast majority were poor Jews who found in London a life that was almost as harsh and dismal as the one they had known in their former homes. Without money, skills, or knowledge of the English language, the new immigrants could only wander up and down the dirty and narrow streets of the poorer sections of the East End, hawking ragged old clothes or lemons or needles and bits of thread. Some of their children were engaged in less savory lines of business. They became pickpockets, or fences for stolen goods.

The established Jewish community, of which Mr. Lyon was proud to be a member, was overwhelmed by the magnitude of the problem. It hadn't helped that many of the wealthier Jewish families had moved out of the area and maintained only tenuous ties with their former synagogues, which were the focal point of traditional Jewish life and provided most of the community's services for the poor. Mr. Lyon knew that he had no right to judge them, for the Talmud itself said that a person had no right to judge another until he had stood in that person's place. And yet he couldn't help but think that the money spent on a lavish dinner party to entertain a Royal Duke could be better spent on helping out a young person recently arrived on English shores. However, this was neither the time nor the place to engage in a lengthy consideration of London's immigrant problem, he reminded himself, as he had work to do.

"Simon, please take this to Mr. Abramson." Mr. Lyon handed a note to a boy of about eight years of age, who had been sitting by the back door of the room, whittling a piece of wood with a small knife. "And make sure you go straight to the warehouse, Simon. Mr. Abramson must receive this message before he locks up the warehouse for the evening."

"Yes, Mr. Lyon."

"After you've delivered it, have your tea and go

to the orphanage. That will be all for today."

The boy tipped his cap and darted out the door, which led to an alley that should, under the proper circumstances, take the child to the warehouse in less than two minutes. However, the streets of London were dangerous and temptation lurked in every alleyway. Simon's parents had both died of consumption within a year of their arrival in England, and so he had been placed in the community's orphanage. But the child had been lured away by a young Jewish troublemaker who promised unsuspecting orphans a life of freedom and full stomachs, if they joined his band of pickpockets. Fortunately, Simon had been rescued from the band's clutches, and Mr. Lyon had volunteered to give the boy employment in his shop as a messenger. Mr. Lyon also made sure that the child received a good dinner in the afternoon and something for his tea before he went to bed. He had also promised Simon that if he performed his duties well, he would be promoted to a more responsible job in the warehouse, where the clocks were manufactured and stored.

Simon had seemed happy with all this, but one never knew what was really going on in the hearts of these children, who had experienced so much hardship in their young lives. And so Mr. Lyon said a silent prayer that the One Above should protect the lad from harm and lead him on the straight path.

He then turned his attention to his account book.

The notes he had sent round to his customers with outstanding debts had resulted in some payments, but not as many as he had hoped. Many of the landed gentry had already left London for Brighton. When the summer resort season ended, they would head to the country, where they would spend the winter visiting each other's country estates. Most wouldn't return to London until the spring, when the London season would begin anew — and when Mr. Lyon would have another chance to request payment.

The bankers and wealthy stockbrokers were in London all year round, but their payments had become less reliable due to the financial markets, which had become topsy-turvy because of the war. No sooner had the English found a way to circumvent Napoleon's blockade on the Continent than the Americans had slapped a trade embargo on English imports. To make up for the loss of trade with England's former colonies, new markets were supposed to open up in South America. But then the Americans rescinded their embargo and suddenly, even without South America, there were more imports and exports than the English traders knew what to do with.

Mr. Lyon didn't know what to do with any of this, either, and he would have much preferred to just mind his own business in his shop on

Cornhill, rather than worry about the business being done on the Continent and in the Americas, North and South. His own first foray into the Stock Exchange had ended badly. He had gambled heavily on the rising price of cotton upon the advice of a stockbroker acquaintance who had assured him that cotton was the safest investment on the Exchange. Mr. Lyon lost his entire investment overnight when the price of cotton unexpectedly fell. He could therefore understand why several of his clients connected with the Royal and Stock Exchanges were unable to pay their bills. These troublesome imports and exports were causing trouble for everyone, from the wealthy bankers who owned fine townhouses on Piccadilly to more modest merchants such as Mr. Lyon, clockmaker, of Cornhill and Devonshire Square.

He set aside the account book and bent down to remove a piece of a floorboard under his desk. This was the place where he hid his locked strongbox, which was where he kept his cash. After lifting up the strongbox and replacing the floorboard, he removed a key from his waistcoat pocket and unlocked the metal box. It was filled with coins and banknotes.

There was too much money in it to be left in the shop, even if the strongbox was carefully stowed in its hiding place. He knew this, but he didn't know what to do with the money as he was uncertain as to how to invest it. He most certainly was not going to invest more of his fortune in the Stock Exchange, so the most sensible place to go was to his bank, a reputable Cornhill establishment managed by Messrs. Smyth, Frye & Co. And normally Mr. Lyon would have taken the contents of his strongbox to this bank at once. However, several banks had recently gone bankrupt and so on this particular day a nagging fear in his heart told him that the banks weren't much better than the Stock Exchange.

"If only that fellow Napoleon would stop with his nonsense, perhaps the markets would settle down," Mr. Lyon muttered unhappily.

"Excuse me, Mr. Lyon."

Mr. Lyon quickly shut the strongbox. He saw that his assistant was standing in the doorway that led in from the showroom of the shop. "Yes, Mr. Warburg?"

"A gentleman wishes to speak with you. Mr. Percy Grenville."

That was the younger son of Lord Grenville, the fifth Earl of Edmonton, and Mr. Lyon couldn't help but show his surprise. "Please tell Mr. Grenville that I shall be with him immediately."

"Yes, Mr. Lyon."

Isaac Warburg went back into the showroom, and Mr. Lyon quickly locked the strongbox. However, instead of returning the box to its hiding place, he thrust it inside a drawer in his desk. Then he straightened his cravat, and went into the showroom.

"Mr. Grenville, this is an unexpected honor."

The young nobleman — who had been examining an ornate musical mantle clock fashioned from Brazilian rosewood that was playing a charming and chiming melody, as the hour was six o'clock in the evening, precisely — removed the quizzing glass from his eye and turned to greet Mr. Lyon.

"I can assure you that this visit is quite unexpected for me, as well, Lyon. I thought to already be in Brighton this evening. However, my father wished me to take care of some business for him before I left town."

Mr. Grenville removed a rather large leather pouch from his coat pocket and gingerly placed it on the counter, as though the pouch's contents might soil his perfectly manicured hands.

"I'm most grateful," Mr. Lyon replied. Of course, he couldn't count out the coins in the pouch in front of the Earl's son, but his eye sized up the size and weight of the pouch and he thought the sum inside was accurate. "I am sorry, though, that you put yourself to so much trouble. I could have come to Lord Grenville's house if he had informed me that he wished to pay me today for the furniture."

"It is a great deal of trouble you've put me to," said the young nobleman, as he removed a gold snuffbox from his other coat pocket and took some snuff. "That tall clock you sold my father has stopped ticking. When the Earl of Edmonton orders an eight-day clock, he does not expect it to rest on the seventh day — even if the clock was made by tradesmen who are idle on Saturdays."

Mr. Lyon, of course, did not reply to that slight against Jews who stubbornly continued to observe the Jewish Sabbath. Instead, he said, "I shall come to inspect the clock at Lord Grenville's earliest convenience."

"No, you shall not. We have already closed up the house for the season. I have therefore brought the thing here."

"Here?"

"It's waiting in back."

"But this is just the shop. The warehouse is at the other end of the alley."

"Really, Lyon, you don't expect me to go wandering through the back alleys of the East End with a tall clock that doesn't tick, do you?"

"Of course not, Mr. Grenville. I only meant that if you would allow me to escort your servants to the correct building..."

"My servants do not have the time, because I do not have the time. And if your clock had the time, I would already be in Brighton. Would you therefore show my servants where they may deposit the clock?"

"Yes, Mr. Grenville. At once."

Mr. Lyon was so flustered that he completely forgot about the pouch lying on the counter. He quickly went into the back room to open the door for the servants. After much maneuvering, for the clock was large and the doorway was small, the two servants finally managed to drag the longcase clock inside. Then, their job finished, they quickly left.

When Mr. Lyon returned to the showroom, Mr. Grenville had left, as well.

"The money!" Mr. Lyon cried out, when he saw the counter and realized that the pouch was gone.

"I have it," said Mr. Warburg, as he removed the pouch from under the counter. "I don't care if that Mr. Grenville is the son of an Earl. There is something about that man that I don't trust."

Mr. Lyon didn't say anything. He took the pouch and returned to the back room. After counting out the heavy coins, he made a notation in his account book. The Earl of Edmonton had recently remodeled his London townhouse and bought several clocks — both longcase and mantle clocks — for the various rooms. Now the bill was paid in full. Mr. Lyon was grateful for that, but he really would have to do something about all the money sitting in the cashbox. In the meantime, he put the box back in its hiding place and replaced the floorboard, and then he went to get his hat.

"Mr. Warburg, I shall be at Baer's Coffee House,

should anyone else inquire for me."

"Yes, Mr. Lyon," Mr. Warburg replied.

Mr. Lyon did not have to explain. Everyone knew that Baer's Coffee House was the place to go when a person had a question or a problem. Someone there was bound to have some good advice about what to do with a nice sum of money. And if they didn't know, they would know who to ask.

Before leaving, Mr. Lyon glanced over at the longcase clock. Despite what Mr. Percy Grenville had said — for Mr. Lyon was sure that the mechanical difficulty could be easily repaired — the clock was one of his finest achievements. The clock was taller and wider than the usual clock, because when Lord Grenville had remodeled his library he had expanded the proportions of the room and so the measurements of the clock had been re-proportioned accordingly. This expanded space gave Mr. Lyon's artisans ample room to show off their considerable skills.

The flame red mahogany case, polished until it shone like the setting sun, had a hood that was topped by an unusual pagoda-style structure, for Lord Grenville had an interest in the East. The clock's dial featured a pearly white face offset by delicately filigreed brass hands and clearly drawn Roman numerals all painted in a rich ebony color. The spandrels of the dial featured a cheerful floral display in each of the four corners, while crowning the dial was an arched lunette with a series of three paintings to indicate the progression of the moon as it traveled through its lunar cycle: the smiling face of a demure lunar miss for when the moon was full, a ship sailing on a darkly lit sea to show the pale and waning moon, and a more brightly lit rustic landscape to show the waxing moon gaining strength.

The inner workings of the clock — its system of pendulum and weights — had been designed with the greatest precision, and so it was odd that the clock should malfunction so soon. It was also odd that Lord Grenville had asked his son to bring it over. Usually, because the clocks were so large and heavy, Mr. Lyon sent a few of his workers to the nobleman's townhouse and they did the repair work there. In very rare cases, when the clock had to be completely dismantled and refitted, his workers brought the clock to the warehouse. He couldn't imagine what had made Lord Grenville decide to transport the clock to Mr. Lyon's shop. But there was no accounting for many of the strange things that noblemen did. For instance, he would never understand what pleasure the lords and ladies got from hunting animals, and yet that was how many of them spent the winter months. Mr. Lyon therefore decided to turn his attention away from the clock, which could be dealt with on the morrow, and fix it upon a more pressing matter.

He had a strongbox full of money that needed to be properly disposed of, and so, after locking the back door behind him, he hurried off in the direction of Baer's Coffee House.

Chapter Five

Mr. lyon never arrived at the coffee house. Just as he was about to turn into Sweeting's Alley, the narrow lane where Mr. Baer's venerable establishment was located, he unexpectedly met his former assistant, Mr. Jacob Oppenheim.

"Jacob? What are you doing in London?" he asked.

The young man did not answer at once, and when he did his eyes were fixed upon the display window of a jeweler's shop. "I have some business to do here."

"That means business must be good. But even

a successful merchant must take some refreshment during the day, so come with me to Baer's. I want to hear all about how you are getting on in Manchester."

Once again, Mr. Lyon noticed that his former assistant was avoiding his gaze. "Of course, if you have another engagement, I won't detain you."

"I am sorry, Mr. Lyon. I am not in London for a social visit. Otherwise, I would have come round to the shop. But I am glad to see you. I hear that I must wish you *mazel tov*. Please accept my best wishes. May your daughter's wedding take place at an auspicious hour."

"Amen," said Mr. Lyon, as he watched the young man hurry down the street.

While Mr. Lyon was still puzzling over the strange transformation of his former assistant, who formerly had always greeted him with an open and frank expression, he noticed that a small crowd of men had started to run in the direction of the Royal Exchange. Although he didn't know why, he began to run after them. When they came to the street where the banking establishment of Brickwood & Co. was located, Mr. Lyon saw that a large crowd had formed outside the bank's doors, which were firmly shut. The men at the front of the crowd were banging on the doors and shouting.

"What has happened?" Mr. Lyon asked the man **standing beside** him.

"West India," the man replied.

Mr. Lyon tried to fix the location of West India in his mind. He knew the name referred to a string of islands that lay across the Atlantic Ocean. He also knew that sugar and rum flowed into England from the West India islands that it controlled.

"West India?" Mr. Lyon whispered, sorry for the distress of the man standing beside him, but also secretly grateful that it was not South America, where his own bank was heavily invested.

"Thomas Coles and Sons have gone bankrupt. They were brokers in West India."

"Were they?"

"They've taken the bank with them," said the man as he nodded his head in the direction of the bank's heavy wood doors. His face was quite ashen. "The bank has declared bankruptcy."

"Have they?" Mr. Lyon noticed that beads of sweat had formed on his companion's face.

The man suddenly removed a large packet of banknotes from his pocket and, strangely, started to laugh. Mr. Lyon saw that the banknotes had been issued by Brickwood & Co. If the bank failed, as it looked like it had, the banknotes were worthless. Unlike coins, which were minted by the Crown and accepted as legal tender everywhere, each bank issued its own banknotes. Only the issuing bank could redeem them for cash. They could not be redeemed for cash at any other institution.

"Steady, my good man," said Mr. Lyon. "Surely all is not lost."

The man stared at Mr. Lyon. "Surely it is."

Mr. Lyon was not exactly sure what happened next, but somehow he found himself engaged in an awesome struggle with this heretofore stranger, who had removed a dangerous looking dagger from his coat pocket and seemed determined to thrust it into his heart. Mr. Lyon was equally determined to prevent the man from taking his own life. He was aware that a crowd was watching them, and he dearly wished that someone would come to his assistance. But no one did. However, just when Mr. Lyon felt his own strength ebbing, for the ruined man had on his side the superhuman strength of the truly desperate, a man burst through the crowd and grabbed the dagger from the would-be suicide's hand.

"Mr. Melamed!" Mr. Lyon cried out with surprise. "Thank G-d you're here!"

"And thank G-d you were here, Mr. Lyon," replied Ezra Melamed, who still had the bankrupted man in his grip. "Do you know this man?"

"No, I don't."

"Well, I'll take him round to Baer's for a talk and a glass of wine," said Mr. Melamed, as he handed the dagger to Mr. Lyon while he searched through the man's coat pockets for the dagger's protective sheath. After he had found the sheath and put the dagger safely away, he said to Mr. Lyon, "You look like you could use something to steady your nerves, yourself."

Mr. Lyon was aware that his hands were shaking, but he was no longer in a frame of mind to engage in conversation in the coffee house. And as the ruined man seemed to have lost all powers of resistance once the weapon had been taken from him, Mr. Lyon was sure that Mr. Melamed would be able to handle the situation on his own. Furthermore, along with the talk and the wine, Mr. Melamed would most likely provide the unfortunate man with some financial assistance, and such things were better done without a third party looking on.

"I rather think I would like to go home," Mr. Lyon therefore replied.

"My carriage is across the street. Tell my coachman to take you to Devonshire Square and return to Sweeting's Alley in an hour."

"Thank you."

Mr. Lyon gave a parting look to the man whose life he had so recently saved. He was sure he had done the right thing. However, his blood ran cold as he studied the man's deathly pale face. To be without money in London was not a fate to be envied.

❖ ❖ ❖

"MUST YOU GO OUT THIS evening, Hannah?" Mrs. Lyon asked.

"There's to be a special tea for the children at the orphanage. I have helped to make all the arrangements. I must be there."

"But you look so tired."

"It's just a summer cold, Mama. Please don't worry. Rebecca, are you ready?"

Rebecca put aside her book, and put on her bonnet. Meshullam Mendel, their male servant, who was married to Sorel, their cook (they were the parents of Perl, the family's maid), was waiting at the door. He would escort the two Miss Lyons to the orphanage, as respectable young ladies could not walk through the East End streets alone.

As they were leaving, they met Mr. Lyon, who had just come home.

"There's a special tea for the children in the orphanage," Hannah said in reply to his quizzical look.

Mr. Lyon did not say it, but he was much relieved. He wished to have a quiet evening, and that would be accomplished more easily if his two eldest daughters had their tea outside the home. However, he did not find the peace he sought in the undisturbed privacy of his library. His uneasy thoughts kept wandering from his strongbox in his shop to his investments in his bank, and from the islands in West India to the **countries of South America.**

The clock chimed nine, ten, eleven, and twelve, but still he continued to pace up and down the room. By the time it chimed five, he had come to a decision: He would exchange his banknotes for solid English guineas. He would then ask Mr. Melamed for advice as to how to invest the money in real estate. London was growing at an astounding pace. Mr. Melamed's family had made their fortune in land speculation. Therefore, surely Mr. Melamed would know about outlying areas that still could be bought at a reasonable price.

Although his plan brought him some relief, Mr. Lyon still continued to pace up and down the room. Every few minutes he glanced out the window, impatiently searching for signs of the rising sun. He had to remove his money from the bank before it was too late.

✦ ✦ ✦

THE REST OF THE FAMILY was already seated around the breakfast table when Perl discovered Mr. Lyon asleep in the library.

"Begging your pardon, Mr. Lyon, I didn't know you were here."

"What time is it, child?"

"Almost nine."

Mr. Lyon sprang from his chair and went over to the window. The sunlit square showed him that the maid was correct. He rushed to his room to wash his face and put on fresh clothes. He wanted to run straight to the bank, but his conscience prevented him from doing so. It was too late to attend the Morning Service at the Great Synagogue, but that was no excuse for not taking the time to pray at home. He therefore donned his *tallis* and *tefillin* — the traditional prayer shawl and phylacteries worn by Jewish men — and opened his prayer book, and chanted the familiar words of the Morning Service.

When he had finished — and to be truthful, his thoughts had been too scattered to pray with the concentration required, even though he knew that he was sorely in need of the mercies of the One Who answers all prayers — he opened the safe in his library and removed all the banknotes in his possession, which he stuffed into the pocket of his greatcoat.

Without so much as tasting his breakfast, he said good-bye to his surprised family — before they could ask why he was in such a hurry or why he was wearing a heavy coat on such a warm day — and rushed out the door. His family would have been further surprised to see him hail a carriage, for Mr. Lyon usually walked to his shop when the weather was fine, as he considered it to be excellent exercise. However, on this morning speed was the greater virtue.

The   carriage   passed   Houndsditch   and

Camomile Streets and turned onto Bishopsgate, a wide thoroughfare lined with shops, as well as several banks, including Mr. Lyon's bank, Smyth, Frye & Co. If he had not been able to summon up the necessary strength of mind to pray earlier, Mr. Lyon found that his mind had suddenly become wonderfully focused.

"Please, Hashem," he softly murmured, as the carriage slowly traveled down the busy street, "let my bank be open for business. Let everything be as usual."

However, as the carriage neared the turnoff for Threadneedle Street, the already crowded thoroughfare became even more congested. Throngs of people had congregated in front of a certain building and their number was so great that they blocked the greater portion of the street. There was no mistaking the angry tone of the men's voices as they shouted to the persons who were presumably inside the red brick building, whose windows and shutters were tightly shut.

"Stop the carriage," Mr. Lyon hoarsely whispered to the coachman.

As if in a dream, where time has slowed down to almost a standstill, he reached into his waistcoat pocket and pulled out a coin, which he handed to the driver. Still as if in a dream, he jumped down from the carriage and walked to the outer edge of the crowd. And still as if in a dream, only this time it was as if he was in a dream that he had seen himself dream before, he heard himself ask, slowly, "What has happened?"

"South America," the man standing next to him slowly replied.

"South America?"

"They've declared bankruptcy," the man said, as he slowly nodded his head in the direction of the tightly shuttered building.

"South America?"

"No. Smyth, Frye & Co. The whole lot of them. A rotten business this is, that's what I say. The government ought to step in and do something, before every bank in London fails."

The man left. Mr. Lyon somehow managed to rouse himself from his dream-like state and extricate himself from the crowd, which was growing larger and angrier by the minute. He hurried down Bishopsgate and quickened his pace even further when he reached the turnoff to Cornhill. From there, he almost ran all the way to his shop. He was ruined, yes, but not penniless. He was not like the man yesterday who had lost everything, he tried to reassure himself. He still had the money in the strongbox.

When he reached his shop, he flung open the door and raced to the back room. Although he couldn't explain why, he had become seized with the need to hold the coins sitting in the strongbox in his hand. He needed to hang onto something solid — good English coins that would be honored in a butcher's shop or a bakery; good English coins that would stave off the pain and the humiliation of sudden poverty; good English coins that would keep him and his family out of debtors' prison, at least for a little while.

"Please, Hashem, don't let it come to that!" he whispered as he bent down underneath his desk. His arm was already outstretched and prepared to rip off the floorboard when he saw that someone had spared him the trouble. The floorboard was not there. The hiding place was uncovered. With a trembling hand, he reached inside the hole in the floor. The hole was not large, and so it only took his fingers a few moments to explore the entire space. It was empty.

Slowly, he raised himself up to a standing position. He stumbled toward the showroom of his shop, clutching his chest, in desperate need of air.

"Mr. Lyon! Are you not feeling well?" asked Mr. Warburg, who had only just then entered the shop.

Mr. Lyon did not reply, for he had already collapsed onto the floor.

Chapter Six

"HE'LL SURVIVE," SAID THE DOCTOR who had been summoned to attend to Mr. Lyon.

"Thank G-d," said Mr. Warburg.

"And you, sir," the doctor said to Mr. Lyon, who was sitting up, but still feeling weak, "what do you think you were doing, running through the streets of London on such a hot day in that heavy coat? It's no wonder you became overheated and fainted."

Mr. Lyon said nothing. It was better that the doctor think his fainting spell was due to his unfortunate choice of a coat than to reveal the true cause of his discomfort. News traveled fast in London. If word got around that he had been ruined, his creditors would be at his door before the afternoon was out.

"Should I call for a carriage to take you home?" asked Mr. Warburg after the doctor had left.

"No, I'm already feeling much better," Mr. Lyon replied, trying to sound livelier than he felt. "Perhaps, though, I will go to Baer's and have something to eat. A strong cup of coffee will put me back on my feet."

"I'll tell Simon to accompany you," said Mr. Warburg, noticing that Mr. Lyon's walk was not steady. The assistant went into the back room, but when he returned to the showroom it was without the boy. "That's strange. The child was here a few minutes ago. I wonder where he could have gone."

◆ ◆ ◆

THE MORNING RUSH IN BAER'S Coffee House had ended. As Asher Baer, the proprietor of the establishment, surveyed his little kingdom located in Sweeting's Alley, he noted with pleasure that all was in order: The tables had been wiped clean, the dishes had been washed, and the pots used to cook the coffee had been scoured. Everything was ready for the next round of business, which would occur at midday.

"Will you be needing anything else? More

coffee, perhaps?" he asked the sole customer still in the room.

"No, thank you," replied Mr. Ezra Melamed, who was sitting in his usual place, in the back corner of the room, and reading the morning newspaper.

Mr. Baer gave the spotless table a quick wipe down with his towel, out of habit, and then returned to the counter, where he noticed that the sign which announced the rules of his establishment was slightly crooked. All London coffee houses had their rules and regulations, and Baer's Coffee House was no exception:

No ladies allowed inside the premises.
No gambling.
No strong language.
No quarreling.
No consumption of strong drink.
Only food cooked on the premises is allowed to be eaten.

Although the first five rules were common for most coffee houses, the last rule was due to the need to preserve the Jewish dietary laws, which were strictly observed in Asher Baer's coffee house. It would hardly do for someone to place his privately bought wedge of cheese on one of the coffee house's plates that was used for meat.

After straightening the sign, Mr. Baer poured

himself a cup of coffee and picked up a newspaper, even though he really didn't need a newspaper to tell him what was going on in the world. His coffee house, like the other coffee houses in the area, was a magnet for the merchants, stockbrokers, and bankers who did business in the City. Of course, his clientele was a Jewish one, but his coffee house served the same purpose as the others: The small but comfortably furnished room provided a congenial setting for lively debates about whatever subjects had seized the public's attention on that particular day. News was traded about the ups and downs of the Stock Exchange, as well as the war being fought on the Spanish peninsula. Announcements were made concerning births, engagements, and — it shouldn't happen to anyone we know — deaths. In short, it was a place to enjoy the company of like-minded friends and business acquaintances, and Mr. Baer prided himself on providing an invaluable service to the Jewish people with his kosher establishment.

Mr. Baer was also happy that he could provide a service to Ezra Melamed in a more private way. Mr. Melamed had recently lost his wife to a sudden illness — a tragic event that occurred not long after Passover and just a few months after the Melameds married off their second and youngest daughter. When this daughter and her husband moved to America, leaving Mr. Melamed quite alone in London, Mr. Baer opened up his home to the widower. Every Shabbos, Mr. Melamed ate his meals with Asher Baer and his family. And if there are those who are wondering what enjoyment a man of great wealth could feel in the home of a simple coffee house proprietor, they simply do not know Mr. and Mrs. Baer, who are the embodiment of good cheer and friendly hospitality. Furthermore, Miriam Baer is an excellent cook.

Mr. and Mrs. Baer hoped, naturally, that the day would soon come when their esteemed Shabbos guest would once again sit at the head of his own table. And one might have thought that the remarriage of such an eligible man would be an easy matter, for Ezra Melamed, who was only in his late forties, had good health, great wealth, refined manners, and a pleasant appearance to recommend him. Furthermore, his two children were already married and established in their own homes — the elder daughter lived on the European Continent, while the young daughter, as has been mentioned, lived on American shores — and so there was no danger of the children meddling in their father's affairs, which some people say can happen. However, this Narrator has not seen such a thing firsthand and so she cannot express an opinion as to whether or not having children — especially daughters — living at a great distance from their parents would be considered to be another point in Mr. Melamed's favor.

But despite Mr. Melamed's many advantages, our Sages tell us that finding one's marriage partner is as difficult as splitting the Red Sea. Should we be tempted to doubt the truth of their words, G-d forbid, we have only to ask the opinion of a certain Jewish matron living in Sweeting's Alley. For although Mrs. Baer always kept her ears open for news concerning Jewish ladies of quality who had been recently widowed, the lady destined to be Mr. Melamed's second wife had not yet been found.

If Mr. Melamed was privately distressed by his new unmarried status, he did not parade his feelings in public. Perhaps the only indication that he had not been entirely successful in coping with his loss was that he spent more time in the coffee house than had been his custom when he was a happily married man. Therefore, in that summer of 1810, it was not an uncommon occurrence for him to be seated in the back corner, reading his newspaper and drinking his coffee, as he was doing at the moment when Mr. Lyon walked into the establishment.

"Could I trouble Mrs. Baer for a little breakfast, Asher?" asked Mr. Lyon.

Mr. Baer, who was startled by his friend's shaken appearance, rushed to show Mr. Lyon to a table. "It's no trouble at all, Samuel," he replied, and then he hurried up the back stairs to the building's second floor, which served as both his home and the kitchen where Miriam Baer prepared food for the coffee house's customers.

Mr. Lyon, thinking he was alone in the room, for he had not noticed Mr. Melamed sitting in the corner, placed his hat on the table and then laid his face upon his hat. He then began to cry.

Mr. Melamed considered what to do. He decided that Mr. Lyon needed this time to express the anguish in his heart, and so he waited. It was only when Mr. Lyon removed a handkerchief from his coat pocket and wiped his face that Mr. Melamed folded his newspaper and put it aside.

"Ah, Mr. Melamed, I did not see you there," said Mr. Lyon, having heard the snap of the paper.

"May I join you? I'm a little hungry myself."

Mr. Lyon motioned for Mr. Melamed to take a seat at his table. "You have seen my tears, and there is no use in either one of us pretending that you did not. This morning, Mr. Melamed, I became one of the synagogue's charity cases."

"You had money invested with Smyth, Frye?"

"My entire fortune. Except for what I had in my shop. I had about a thousand guineas laid away in a strongbox I keep in the back room."

Mr. Melamed could not stop himself from expressing his wonder. "You kept a thousand guineas in your shop?"

"It was foolish of me, I know. But I didn't know

where to invest it. At any rate, it doesn't matter now. The money is gone."

"Gone? I don't understand, Mr. Lyon."

"It seems that someone stole it."

At that moment, Mr. Baer returned to the room with a plate of scrambled eggs and toast. "Here you are, Samuel. You know where to wash your hands."

While Mr. Lyon went to perform the ritual washing of his hands, and while Mr. Baer went to bring two fresh cups of coffee to the table, Mr. Melamed pondered the distressing news he had just heard. Banks failing was not something new. Petty crime carried out in the crowded streets of London also was not something new. But that someone should have had his shop broken into and his money stolen was new, at least for the Jewish merchants that he was acquainted with, and he hoped that this was not the beginning of a disturbing trend.

Mr. Lyon returned to the table. After reciting the blessing over eating bread and taking a first bite, he placed the piece of toast back on his plate, unable to eat more. He then said, "I hope you don't mind my backing out of our agreement concerning the rooms on Bury Street. My daughter won't need them now. Of course, we shall have to break off the engagement."

Although he tried not to, Mr. Lyon once again

broke into tears. Mr. Baer, who had brought the coffee, was about to say something, but Mr. Melamed motioned for him to be silent.

"It doesn't matter if Asher knows," said Mr. Lyon. "Soon everyone will know that I've lost all my money."

Mr. Baer gasped. Again he was about to say something, but Mr. Melamed spoke first, saying, "There is no need for anyone to know, except the three of us."

"And you can count on me, Samuel. I won't say a word," Mr. Baer added.

"But I must inform Mr. Goldsmith," said Mr. Lyon. "It would not be fair to not apprise him of my change in fortune."

"Everything can change in a blink of an eye," said Mr. Melamed. "We have time to find the money that has been stolen from you."

"But there were only a thousand guineas in the strongbox," protested Mr. Lyon.

"How much did you promise for your daughter's dowry?" Mr. Baer asked.

"A thousand guineas."

"So there you have it," said Mr. Baer. "If you get back your money, the wedding can take place as planned. Like Mr. Melamed says, no one ever needs to know anything about this."

"But what about the rest of my family?" Mr. Lyon again protested. "What are we to live on?"

When neither Mr. Melamed nor Mr. Baer replied, Mr. Lyon continued to speak. "The situation is hopeless, I tell you. Even with the dowry, Mr. Goldsmith will not wish to be connected with a family whose primary residence is Newgate Prison, debtors' ward. It's better to put an end to the engagement now, before he hears about this from others."

There was another silence, and then it was the turn of Mr. Melamed to protest, which he did quite strongly. "And I say to you, Mr. Lyon, it is forbidden to despair. Do you hear me? You must not give up hope. Therefore, I repeat, do not tell a soul that your fortune was invested with Smyth, Frye. As for the burglary, after you've finished your breakfast, I will accompany you to your shop. Perhaps the thief left something behind that we can use to trace his identity."

"No. I cannot allow you to become involved in this, Mr. Melamed. It was wrong of me to take advantage of your kind heart and burden you with my troubles."

"Mr. Lyon, my interest in your affairs has nothing to do with having a kind heart. As one of the trustees of the Great Synagogue, and someone who both contributes to and oversees the charitable fund, I can tell you that this fund is already taxed to its limit. I therefore cannot afford to let criminals break into the shops of Jewish merchants and rob them of their fortunes, and thereby add more names to the charity's rolls. My involvement in this venture is due solely to my duty to the synagogue and the community, and you have no right to prevent me from performing this duty."

Mr. Lyon didn't believe a word of Mr. Melamed's fine speech. If it were simply a matter of trying to find the thief, they could refer the matter to the Bow Street Runners, professional thief-apprehenders who worked for the Magistrate's office on Bow Street. However, Mr. Lyon did not protest further, since he was grateful for this offer of assistance.

"What do I owe you, Asher, for the breakfast?" asked Mr. Lyon, as he reached a finger into his waistcoat pocket, hoping that he still had a few coins in it.

"Not a farthing. This was a breakfast between friends, as if you had eaten it upstairs and at my own table."

"Nonsense," said Mr. Melamed. "Mr. Lyon does not need anyone's charity. Keep a strict account of everything that he eats and drinks in your coffee house, because he is going to pay you back every last penny, with Hashem's help."

Chapter Seven

MR. MELAMED STARED UP AT the small window. It was situated to the right of the door that led to the alley in back of Mr. Lyon's shop. Besides being small, it was high up and had iron bars. It therefore wasn't likely that the thief had entered the shop through it. But since he wished to make a thorough examination of the room, Mr. Melamed moved a crate over to the back wall and climbed onto the crate. He could now easily reach the window and test the bars, which he did. The bars were securely affixed to the window's casing. Disappointed, he stepped down from the crate.

He was by no means a professional investigator,

but the subject of solving crimes had always interested him. But then solving any intellectual puzzle interested him, which was one of the reasons why he enjoyed learning Talmud. And as his gaze shifted from the small window to the back room's door and from there to the door that led to the showroom, a puzzle from the Talmud came to mind:

What is the law if a mouse enters a house with a piece of bread in its mouth and a mouse leaves with a piece of bread in its mouth? Do we say that the mouse that entered is the one that left, or perhaps it is a different mouse?

The question was posed by a Talmudic Sage called Rava in *Pesachim* 10b, the volume of the Talmud that discusses the laws of the Passover holiday. In this instance, the Sages were discussing the laws of searching a house for *chametz* after the house had already been cleaned — *chametz* being the unleavened bread which a Jew is forbidden to eat or own during the holiday. If it was the same mouse, Rava asked, can we assume that there was no *chametz* in the house — that the *chametz* in the mouse's mouth when it left was the same *chametz* it had brought into the house from the outside — and so the house need not be cleaned again? Or, if there were two mice, should we assume that the mouse that leaves with the piece of bread in his **mouth found the bread inside the house, and so** the house must be cleaned and searched anew?

It was an interesting question to ponder. However, Mr. Melamed wasn't sure why it had snuck into his mind at this particular moment. Unless, of course, it was because of the fact that the strongbox had obviously been stolen, but there were no signs of anyone having forced his way into Mr. Lyon's shop. So was the "mouse" that left with the strongbox the same "mouse" that entered the shop with a key? Or were there two different "mice"?

"Are you sure that no one has a key to the shop except you and Mr. Warburg?" he asked.

"There is a third key, which I keep in my desk drawer." Mr. Lyon opened the drawer to show Mr. Melamed the key. His face assumed a puzzled expression. "It's not here."

"And it was there yesterday?"

Mr. Lyon thought for a moment. "Yes, I saw it."

"Was this back door locked when you came to the shop this morning?"

"I don't know. I believe I locked it last night, before I left. But this morning I entered through the front door of the shop and came straight to the desk."

"So you did not unlock it?"

"No."

"Could Mr. Warburg have unlocked it?"

"I suppose so. I fainted, you see, so I don't know

what happened while I was unwell. However, after I recovered he did come in here to look for Simon. Apparently the boy had been here earlier, but had left."

"He left through this door?"

"Of course. Simon is not allowed to use the front door of the shop."

"Then the door must have been unlocked by the time Simon arrived here this morning."

"Yes, I suppose so."

Mr. Melamed continued to examine the door's lock. Although he would have preferred to believe that the theft had been committed by someone who had no connection to the shop, the evidence seemed to say otherwise, since there were no signs of the lock having been forced.

"Mr. Lyon, I'd like to borrow your key for a moment, and ask Mr. Warburg a few questions."

"You're going to tell him, then, about the theft?"

"No. I'm just going to ask some questions."

Mr. Lyon handed his key to Mr. Melamed, who entered the shop's showroom. As there were no customers there at the moment, Mr. Warburg was dusting the mantle clocks that were on display. He turned when Mr. Melamed entered the room.

"Business is slow, I see, Mr. Warburg."

"It usually is at this hour. The gentry are still having their breakfast, while the brokers are making their deals at the Exchange."

"Mr. Lyon gave us quite a scare this morning, didn't he?"

"Yes, he did. But I trust he is feeling better?"

"I believe he is. By the way, I found this key lying on the floor of the back room. You must have dropped it after you unlocked the back door this morning. Accidents do happen, and so I shan't mention it to Mr. Lyon, but do try to be more careful in the future."

Mr. Warburg looked at the key that was sitting in the palm of Mr. Melamed's hand. Then he reached into his waistcoat pocket and pulled out an identical key.

"I have my key, Mr. Melamed. And I believe it was Mr. Lyon who opened the back door, as he usually does. Perhaps the key fell out of Mr. Lyon's pocket when he became ill."

"Ah, I hadn't thought of that. Of course, that's what must have happened."

Mr. Melamed then turned his attention to one of the mantle clocks, as though he was interested in making a purchase. "Is this the musical clock with the new chiming mechanism?" he asked.

"No, sir, this is the one," Mr. Warburg replied, as he pointed to the clock that had caught the attention of Mr. Percy Grenville the previous day.

Mr. Melamed studied the clock for a few **minutes, and then he said, "Consider it sold. I shall** discuss the payment details with Mr. Lyon."

"Yes, sir."

Mr. Melamed returned to the back room, and gave the key to Mr. Lyon. He correctly assumed that Mr. Lyon had overheard the entire conversation, and so he did not repeat it.

"You don't have to buy the clock, Mr. Melamed."

"No, I don't. But it's a stunning piece of work and I do need a new clock for my library. Now let's get back to this mystery of yours."

"I am sure you will agree with me that Mr. Warburg did not commit the crime," said Mr. Lyon.

"I haven't ruled out anyone yet. There is still the matter of the third key. Perhaps he was not working alone."

"No, I am certain he wasn't involved."

"How can you be so sure?"

"I have been in business for many years, and I believe I have the ability to judge a man's character. Mr. Warburg is a married man with an infant son. He has shown himself to be a reliable and hard-working assistant, eager to support his family and advance himself in the world. If he were capable of committing such a despicable act, I am sure I would have suspected something."

Mr. Melamed thought back to the events of the day before, which Mr. Lyon had related to him as they returned to the shop. "Yet you did suspect him of taking the pouch filled with Lord Grenville's money."

"No, that's not true. I was merely momentarily worried that something had happened to the money. I didn't have time to suspect anyone, for Mr. Warburg immediately produced the pouch, which he had prudently placed under the counter."

Mr. Melamed wanted to agree with Mr. Lyon's assessment of the young immigrant's character, but, unfortunately, Mr. Warburg was the man who was the most likely to have committed the crime. He saw Mr. Percy Grenville pay the outstanding bill, and so he would have known there was something in the strongbox worth stealing. He also had a key to the shop, and so he could have easily removed the strongbox and taken it with him when he locked up the shop for the night. No one on the busy street would have noticed him carrying the box, and if they had there was no way to find those people now.

The only question was, when Mr. Warburg had so much time to commit the crime, why didn't he replace the floorboard? Or if he wished the theft to appear to be the result of someone breaking into the shop, why didn't he create more of a disorder? A clever man — and Mr. Warburg struck him as being a man of intelligence — would have made the burglary look like it was an outside job. He would have turned over the desk chair, flung some paper onto the floor, and left a drawer open to make it appear as though the thief had to search for the money.

Yes, that was the other thing that was odd about this crime, Mr. Melamed realized. Not only did the thief have no trouble getting inside the shop, but he also knew exactly where to look. Who else, besides Mr. Warburg, would satisfy those two requirements?

He didn't like to consider the possibility, but he supposed he had to. The orphan boy, Simon, could have easily slipped into the back room of the shop when no one was there and removed the key. Then he could have returned later that night, after everyone else had gone home, and stolen the box. Or he could have given the third key to his pickpocket friends and they could have done the job.

"Did you ever remove the strongbox while the boy was in this room?" asked Mr. Melamed.

"Never. Does not our Torah tell us that it is forbidden to place a stumbling block in front of the blind?"

"So you do believe that the child is capable of committing an act of theft?"

"A child who is alone in the world might be tempted to do many things to secure his future. But Simon is a good boy. I know it. He wouldn't do anything dishonest on his own."

"However, you did say that he was friendly with some pickpockets. What's the name of their leader? Sir something or other?"

"The Earl of Gravel Lane."

Mr. Melamed smiled. Although he highly disapproved of a Jewish boy engaging in a life of crime, and luring other youngsters into it, as well, he did have to salute the audacity of the "Earl." Jews did not enjoy full civil liberties in England, and no Jew had ever received a peerage. Yet this pickpocket had already proclaimed himself a member of the English aristocracy, and an earl at that.

However, locating his "peerage" in Gravel Lane was troubling. That narrow street was crowded with criminals, including the notorious Ikey Solomon, who had been found guilty of stealing a purse and forty pounds the previous month. Ikey Solomon was presently sitting in a floating prison, awaiting deportation. Mr. Melamed hoped that this Earl of Gravel Lane was not intending to usurp Ikey Solomon's now vacant place.

"I shall want to speak with Simon," said Mr. Melamed. "And the Earl."

Mr. Lyon nodded his head. "I am sure you will find Simon in the warehouse. Unless Mr. Abramson has sent him on an errand."

Mr. Melamed wished he could share the shop **owner's certainty. But even as he wondered about** the orphan boy, the mention of the warehouse manager's name aroused a whole new set of suspicions. "What about this warehouse manager of yours? Could he have taken the third key? Did he know where you hid the strongbox?"

Mr. Lyon didn't answer at once. In the back of his mind, he thought that Mr. Abramson might have something to do with the theft. A few years earlier, the man had been the proprietor of his own clock-making shop and one of Mr. Lyon's competitors. That competition had ended when he went bankrupt after extending too much credit to his fashionable customers. Mr. Lyon had given him a job overseeing the manufacturing process of his own business, a decision he sometimes regretted, as there had always been an unspoken tension between the two men. Should he say anything about this to Mr. Melamed, he wondered?

"He doesn't come here," said Mr. Lyon, still undecided as to what he should say and what was best left unspoken. "When I need to speak with him, I go to the warehouse. However, he must have known that I keep some cash on hand, since he once owned a shop, himself. Bills do sometimes come up which need to be paid immediately."

"I remember his shop. I bought a few pieces from him. It must be hard for him to work under someone else."

"But that doesn't mean he would stoop to theft,"

replied Mr. Lyon, realizing that it was foolish to hide anything from Mr. Melamed. They were both from the same community. They both knew who got along and who bore a grudge.

"And this former assistant of yours? The one you said you met last evening? Could he stoop to theft?"

"Jacob Oppenheim? Oh, no, Mr. Melamed. Mr. Oppenheim could not have committed such a crime."

"Why not?"

"Why, for any number of reasons. He worked for me for five years and never once did he give me reason to question his honesty. And he is an outstanding Torah scholar. And he wouldn't have known that I had a large sum of money in the shop. That was not my usual practice when he was employed by me. And we met last evening quite by chance. He wasn't even intending to pay me a visit, because he was so pressed for time."

"And yet he would not tell you why he was so pressed for time, correct?"

"I am sorry, but I absolutely refuse to include Jacob's name in your list of suspects."

"Very well," said Mr. Melamed. He didn't want to argue with the merchant, but he, for one, had not crossed out the name of Jacob Oppenheim from his own mental list. "But if the crime wasn't committed by Mr. Oppenheim or Mr. Warburg or

Mr. Abramson or Simon, then it must have been committed by Lord Grenville."

"Surely you are joking, Mr. Melamed."

"We have to consider everyone who could have possibly done it."

"But Lord Grenville is a fabulously wealthy man."

"And his younger son?"

"One does hear things, but so many of the young gentlemen today run up large gambling debts. And why would Percy Grenville have given me the money if he only intended to steal it? He could have told his father that he had been robbed before he got to Cornhill."

"Very true. And it is also true that you are a generous man, Mr. Lyon. In your eyes, no one is guilty. Such an attitude will assure you a place in Heaven, but it won't get you back your thousand guineas."

Mr. Melamed put on his hat and prepared to leave.

"Have you given up, then?" asked Mr. Lyon.

"Given up? My dear Mr. Lyon, you have given me new employment, which is like giving a man a new life, and for that I am grateful. I shan't give up until those guineas of yours are found."

Mr. Melamed closed the back door and left the shop through the front entrance, after tipping his hat to Mr. Warburg. However, instead of continuing down Cornhill Street, he circled round to the narrow alleyway in back of the shop. He wanted to see if he could look inside the shop from the small window, to determine if someone — an outsider — might have spied upon Mr. Lyon unobserved. However, he could only succeed in doing so by jumping up and down, an action which made him feel self-conscious and foolish. He supposed that someone might have dragged over a crate, as he had done inside the shop, but he doubted it. Even though the alley was not a busy street like Cornhill, laborers and tradesmen did pass through it from time to time, and so surely an intelligent thief would not allow himself to be caught performing such a suspicious act.

As Mr. Melamed mulled over his conversation with Mr. Lyon, he remained convinced that the thief, whoever he was, had to possess two things: A key to the shop and the knowledge that the strongbox was hidden under the floorboard.

The ancient riddle posed by Rava began to once again rattle inside his brain: What is the law if a mouse enters a house with a piece of bread in its mouth and a mouse leaves with a piece of bread in its mouth? Do we say that the mouse that entered is the one that left, or perhaps it is a different mouse?

Who entered with the key? Who left with the money? And was there just one person involved, or two?

Chapter Eight

MR. MELAMED DECIDED TO BEGIN his inquiries with Mr. Abramson. As he walked down the narrow alleyway that connected the shop to the warehouse, he further decided upon the pretext he would use to engage Mr. Abramson in conversation. He would ask if the warehouse was in need of more workers. It was a plausible question. As a trustee of the Great Synagogue, and one of its financial supporters, he was very involved with the challenges facing the community, including the problem of finding employment for the new immigrants.

However, despite the virtues of the topic, his

question did not elicit a friendly reply.

"You should speak to Mr. Lyon," Mr. Abramson said sullenly. "He's the owner, not me."

"Yes, I know. But he has an important appointment in the West End, and so he said I should ask you, since you are the one who oversees the workers and manages the warehouse."

Mr. Melamed kept his eyes fixed upon the former shop owner's face. If the man was afflicted with the negative trait of false pride, as his initial sullenness implied, it would irk him to be reminded that he had been demoted to the warehouse, while it was Mr. Lyon who visited well-to-do customers in their fashionable townhouses. However, Mr. Abramson's face was, curiously, a cipher.

"But business is good, I hope?" Mr. Melamed continued. "Perhaps you need a few more clockmakers, or carpenters?"

"Business is not good, Mr. Melamed. I barely have enough work for the men that we have employed here already."

Mr. Abramson nodded toward the work area of the large room. About a dozen men were seated at the two long tables. One of the men was apparently skilled at numbering, as he had several clock dials in front of him and he was painting the Roman numerals on their faces. A few others were painting the moonlit scenes on the lunettes. At another table sat the clockmakers, who performed the intricate mechanical work with their delicate tools. Mr. Melamed assumed that the carpentry work for the longcase clocks was done outside, in a courtyard.

He didn't know the workmen personally, but he recognized their faces since he saw them at the Great Synagogue on Shabbos, when everyone gathered for the prayer services. During the week, they would say their daily prayers here, in their place of work, for as their beards and clothing showed, they were Jews from the European Continent who still clung to their religion's commandments and traditions. Mr. Melamed assumed that most of them probably didn't speak more than a few words of English. If it weren't for businesses such as the one owned by Mr. Lyon, he further assumed that it would be difficult for them to find work.

The thought of Mr. Lyon being forced to close down his business, and sending these honest laborers back into the cruel streets of London, made him angry, but he didn't know to where he should direct that anger. It was not the fault of Mr. Lyon or Smyth, Frye & Co. that the market had turned against them. Honest losses were as much a part of doing business as honest profits. Stealing, though, was another matter, and so Mr. Melamed returned his attention to his own work, which was to discover the thief. He suddenly recalled the longcase clock that Lord Grenville had returned to the shop because it had stopped working. Was it a coincidence that it had stopped working at around the same time that the strongbox was stolen? Or was someone trying to sabotage Mr. Lyon's business?

"Yes, it's the end of the London season, isn't it?" said Mr. Melamed, after deciding to try a different tack with Mr. Abramson. "I suppose the roads are already beginning to be clogged with carriages on their way to Brighton."

When Mr. Abramson didn't say anything, Mr. Melamed continued, "It's a pretty place, Brighton. Have you ever been there, Mr. Abramson?"

Mr. Melamed again tried to see if there was any change in the man's face, perhaps a flicker of anger or envy in his eyes. However, the eyes of Mr. Abramson remained stubbornly blank.

"We used to go, because of my son. He liked the sea."

"I suppose it must be hard for him, having to stay in London all summer, because of your changed circumstances."

Mr. Abramson gave Mr. Melamed a cold look. "My son is dead, Mr. Melamed. He was killed last year in Spain, during the Battle of Talavera. His *yahrtzeit* is next month."

Mr. Melamed closed his eyes. He felt like a fool, or worse, for having forgotten. "I'm sorry," he said.

"Well, you had your own loss not so long ago.

Grief can blind a person to the troubles of others." Then Mr. Abramson added, "I know that Mr. Lyon likes to help these new immigrants, but this isn't the time to hire more workers. Our first loyalty has to be to the ones we already have. We have to keep them employed. If Mr. Lyon asks for my advice, that's what I'm going to tell him. I hope you understand."

"I do understand," said Mr. Melamed, "and thank you for giving me your honest opinion."

And he did believe that Mr. Abramson was being honest. Whatever private struggles Mr. Abramson might be going through, he was sure that Mr. Abramson's concern for his workers was sincere and so he wouldn't do anything to harm the business.

"But we may need a new messenger boy."

Mr. Melamed, who had turned to leave, stopped and turned back around. He had forgotten about Simon. "I thought you had a messenger boy. Has something happened to him?"

Mr. Abramson shrugged. "I don't know. I haven't seen him all day."

"Is he usually here in the morning?"

"Yes, and it's a shame that he wasn't here today. The price of mahogany fell yesterday afternoon. I wanted to send a message to the timber warehouse first thing this morning to place an order. By now, all the wood has probably been purchased by others."

"Well, if you need another boy, Mr. Lyon knows where to find me."

◆ ◆ ◆

WHEN MR. MELAMED RETURNED TO Baer's Coffee House, the establishment had assumed a very different atmosphere. The air fairly rang with the animated murmurings of the crowd that had filled most of the tables. Smyth, Frye & Co. had already been forgotten in the excitement of the news that yet another bank had failed. The situation was turning into a real financial panic, and everyone had their own opinion — which they insisted on voicing, sometimes shouting to be heard over the others who were already speaking — as to what the government should do to save the country from ruin.

Mr. Melamed took his usual place in the back of the room. He listened to the clamoring talk of the crowd for a few minutes, and then he returned his attention to his investigation. He was happy to be able to remove Mr. Abramson from his list. He was sorry, though, that he could not do the same for Simon, at least not yet.

Mr. Baer came to take his order, and he asked for a plate of cold meat. Neither one of them said a word about Mr. Lyon. Mr. Baer did look surprised, though when the gentleman investigator asked, in a low voice, so as not to be heard by anyone except Asher Baer, "Was Jacob Oppenheim here yesterday?"

"Yes, he was," replied Mr. Baer. "He came by last evening."

"Do you know where he is staying?"

"I'll ask Mrs. Baer."

Mr. Melamed smiled. He knew that if anyone would know the whereabouts of an eligible young man, it was Mrs. Baer, who considered matchmaking to be her real vocation in life. She was most likely still disappointed that Jacob Oppenheim had left London before she succeeded in finding a wife for him. And she would not have let Mr. Oppenheim escape from the coffee house without first discovering the address of his lodgings, for one never knew when an eligible young lady might suddenly appear and so one had to be prepared.

When Mr. Baer returned with the plate of cold meat, he gave Mr. Melamed the information that he had requested. However, he then added, "I hope your interest in Mr. Oppenheim has nothing to do with that other business."

"I hope my suspicions are unfounded, as well," replied Mr. Melamed. "But did he say why he came to London?"

"Not that I recall."

"Did he speak about any topic?"

"Yes, he asked to hear what was new in the community. Mrs. Baer told him about your daughter leaving for America, and about Samuel's daughter getting engaged to the Goldsmith boy. Mrs. Baer came down for a few minutes to say hello. She is very fond of Mr. Oppenheim and it is a great mystery to her why such a nice young man has not yet found a wife. She spoke of nothing else for the rest of the evening."

"I am sure it is a great mystery for us all. But was he in a cheerful frame of mind, or did it appear that something was bothering him?"

"I suppose he seemed cheerful enough. But, frankly, I had other things to attend to. Somehow a rag got dropped into the stove and nearly burned the place down. Both Mrs. Baer and I had to rush upstairs to put out the fire. By the time I came back downstairs, he was gone. I suppose he grew tired of waiting and went back to his lodgings and had his meal there. But now if you'll excuse me, I have to get back to my other customers."

"One last question, Asher. Do you recall what time it was when you came downstairs?"

"It was six-thirty. I heard the chimes of that clock over there."

Mr. Baer left and Mr. Melamed turned his attention to his meal. He did not linger over it, though, as he had several calls that he wished to make that afternoon. However, he did linger over this interesting puzzle: Six-thirty was the approximate hour when Mr. Oppenheim met Mr. Lyon at the corner of Sweeting's Alley. If Mr. Oppenheim was hungry, why did he not return with Mr. Lyon to the coffee house and have his meal there, or suggest that they have their meal elsewhere? And if he had had time to speak with Mr. and Mrs. Baer, why did he not have time to speak with Mr. Lyon, who was surely a closer acquaintance? And, the most interesting question of all, what had brought the young man to London?

◆ ◆ ◆

"MR. OPPENHEIM? I'M SORRY, MR. Melamed, but he's already left."

"I hope he did not receive bad news. I understand that he only just arrived in London yesterday."

Mrs. Levy, a widow who was the proprietress of a respectable boarding house on King Street, near the Great Synagogue, did not reply. Her silence was admirable, Mr. Melamed had to admit. Many landladies would have welcomed the opportunity to gossip about their lodgers and speculate about their actions.

"Would it be possible to see the room where he stayed?" he asked. "I know of a person who might need a place to stay for a few weeks."

This wasn't an outright lie. He was aware of many

people who needed a room that was comfortable and clean. Mrs. Levy, who knew of his work with the synagogue, led him up the stairs without suspecting an ulterior motive for his interest.

"It's a back room, and so it doesn't get much sunlight," she was saying, as he quickly glanced around the small room. "But it's a comfortable room, even so, and clean."

Mr. Melamed saw that the landlady had spoken the truth, both about the room's lack of sunlight and its cleanliness. To his disappointment, the room had already been tidied up. Fresh linens were on the bed, and the washing up bowl had been cleaned and dried. Mr. Melamed walked over to the wardrobe and opened its doors, hoping that Mr. Oppenheim had left behind some clue concerning the reason for his visit to London. But the young man had left nothing behind.

"Are your lodgers provided with their own key to the front door, so that they may leave and enter as they please, and without waking you or the servants?" asked Mr. Melamed.

"My lodgers are all respectable gentlemen, Mr. Melamed. They may have a key, if they require one. But this is not an inn for gentlemen who spend their evenings in drinking and gambling and then stumble back to their rooms in the middle of the night, making a ruckus as they trip over the stairs, if that was your question."

"Thank you for setting my mind at ease. I assumed your lodgers are all like Mr. Oppenheim — and I am sorry I missed him. If I'd known earlier that he was in town, I would have stopped by last evening. But perhaps I would have missed him anyway, if he was out last night. I assume he dined with friends."

Mrs. Levy let him assume whatever he wished, for all she said in reply was, "If you've seen the room, Mr. Melamed, I need to get back to my work."

"I'm sorry, Mrs. Levy, I didn't mean to trouble you."

"It was no trouble at all, and if the gentleman you are making inquiries for is seeking a comfortable and quiet room," the landlady continued, as she escorted Mr. Melamed back down the stairs, "he won't find a better one than this."

Mr. Melamed silently agreed. The inn was the model of discretion, and therefore the perfect place to stay for a person in need of that particular service.

Chapter Nine

I**F MR. LYON HAD HIS** hopes that Mr. Oppenheim was not the culprit, Mr. Melamed had hopes of his own. As he headed toward his next stop, the community's orphanage — a small establishment that could house no more than a dozen boys and the same amount of girls, and which was located on Little Duke's Place, near to both Mrs. Levy's inn and the Great Synagogue — he dearly hoped that there he would discover a simple reason for Simon's disappearance from the shop. Perhaps the child had fallen ill, for example. What he most definitely did not want to happen was to discover that the **thief was the orphaned boy, and he was more than** a little surprised by the depth of his emotion.

Suddenly he realized that this theft was no longer just an intellectual puzzle to be enjoyably solved over a cup of coffee or a good dinner. By offering to try and find the thief he had unwittingly taken upon himself an awesome responsibility. Therefore, it was perhaps not surprising that he had become deeply involved in the little drama that was unfolding. The futures of real people were at stake, he realized, as he waited in the vestibule for the head of the orphanage to appear. Should he point his finger in the wrong direction — say, at the orphan — he could ruin that child's life forever. He therefore uttered a silent prayer to the Father of orphans and widows that his inquiries should lead him in the right direction and allow him to be a vessel for doing good and not harm.

"Mr. Melamed, this is a pleasant surprise. What may I do for you? I do hope you will stay for tea."

Mr. Maurice Muller, the orphanage's director, was a small man whose quick movements resembled those of a bird in flight. He had fairly glided down the hallway before landing in front of Mr. Melamed, where he seemed to be perched on one leg, ready to take off again at the slightest command.

"But before you tell me your business, you must see our new curtains in the sitting room. They were made by the Young Ladies of the Great Synagogue

Sewing Circle, and I am sure you will agree that the kind hearts of these young ladies can be seen reflected in every stitch."

Mr. Melamed found himself being escorted into the sitting room, for this was Mr. Muller's way. He swept everyone along with him, and his enthusiasm was such that only an incorrigible curmudgeon would wish to resist him. Mr. Melamed dutifully inspected the new curtains, while further noting that the windows had been recently washed. After complimenting the orphanage director for his excellent upkeep of the building — a compliment which the director insisted rightfully belonged to the orphanage's housekeeper — Mr. Melamed got down to business.

"Mr. Muller, it has come to my attention that one of the boys is not at his place of work. I thought that perhaps he had been taken ill. I am referring to Simon, the child who is employed as a messenger at Mr. Samuel Lyon's shop."

Mr. Muller's face assumed a worried expression. "Simon? Oh, dear."

"He is not here at the orphanage?"

"No, he is not."

"Have you any idea where he might be?"

"No, I do not. But if he has run off again to join the gang of the Earl of Gravel Lane, I take no responsibility for it, Mr. Melamed. As you know, I have informed the trustees of the synagogue more than once that children should be in school during the day. A few hours of religious instruction in the evening is not enough. It is a scandal that these children spend most of their day working. And they most especially should not be sent to work as messengers, where it is their job — their job! — to spend the entire day roaming the streets of London on their own."

Mr. Melamed was most surprised by this outburst. As a wealthy man, and a benefactor of the community, he was accustomed to being treated with deference and respect. But the words of the orphanage director hit their mark, and so instead of replying with words of anger he accepted the rebuke and said, "The community is doing the best that it can, Mr. Muller."

He did not wait to hear Mr. Muller's reply. Even he had his doubts as to whether he had, indeed, spoken the truth.

◆ ◆ ◆

"SEE HERE, SQUIRE, THIS IS private property you're trespassing on."

From behind him, Mr. Melamed heard several children laugh. It had not escaped his notice that a gaggle of youngsters had been following him ever since he left the just passably genteel neighborhood of Duke's Place and crossed over into the decidedly questionable area on the other side of Petticoat Square. Instinctively, his hand went to his coat pocket. It was possible that the children were only curious. It was probable that they hoped to relieve him of his handkerchief, or his money.

As he glanced around the narrow, dingy lane, he wondered who would bother to stake a claim on such a miserable spot. Then he checked himself. If he was to gain the trust of these children, he mustn't look down on them.

"I beg your pardon," he said, as he pulled out his calling card case, which was thankfully still in his possession. He took out one of his cards and presented it to the youngster who had spoken to him and was presently blocking his path.

The boy, who was dressed in an oversized and old-fashioned military coat that dusted the ground and a too-long pair of leather breeches that performed a similar service for his ankles, pushed up the two-cornered bicorne hat that had threatened to fall down upon his nose. Then, having removed this black woolen obstacle from before his eyes, he made a great show of reading the letters printed on the card. After a few moments, though, he stuffed the card into his coat pocket and said, "I left my quizzing glass in my civilian clothes, Squire. Perhaps you'd like to tell me who you are, and what is your business?"

"With pleasure," replied Mr. Melamed. "But

perhaps you would first do me the favor of informing me who I have the honor of speaking with."

"General Well'ngone," the boy said, after removing his hat and making a deep bow. "Right-hand man to his lordship, the Earl of Gravel Lane."

"Mr. Ezra Melamed," replied Mr. Melamed, making a slight bow. "Is the Earl at home, by any chance?"

"Why do you want to know?"

"Maybe his Squireship is tired of the food they serve in the orphanage and would like to dine with the Earl, instead," one of the other boys said with a sneer. The rest of the children laughed.

Mr. Melamed paid them no heed. Instead, he looked the young Well'ngone in the eye and said, "I wish to speak with the Earl of Gravel Lane. You have my card. Please tell him I am here."

Well'ngone returned his gaze. Then he placed his hat upon his head and said, "Watch him, boys, and keep an eye on your handkerchiefs. Bankers and stockbrokers are famous for sticking their hands into other people's pockets and stealing their fortunes."

With that, Well'ngone removed a handkerchief from his own pocket — which Mr. Melamed recognized as being one of his own — and waved it before Mr. Melamed's face.

"This is the sort of calling card we use in Gravel Lane, Squire. It saves us the cost of the ink."

Well'ngone disappeared inside a dark hole of a doorway, leaving Mr. Melamed to ponder the interesting question of how the handkerchief had been removed from the pocket of his coat without his noticing. The other youngsters, who were still gawking and laughing at him, clearly had enjoyed Well'ngone's performance.

As he looked at them, he wondered if Simon was the type of child to be easily taken in by the bravado, as well. He hoped not. These children might be laughing now, but many of them would be caught by the Bow Street Runners one day. If they were lucky, and their judge was feeling kind-hearted, they would be deported to Australia and sentenced to hard labor for a dozen years. If the judge was not so amiably disposed, they would be hanged. Thieves were plentiful in London, and so the court could afford to dispose of them as it pleased.

Well'ngone returned and said, "You're in luck, Squire. The Earl is receiving visitors."

Mr. Melamed was escorted inside the building and led down a shaky and dimly lit flight of stairs. The below-ground area had the unmistakable fragrance of rotting rubbish, but as his handkerchief was no longer in his possession, he could not use it to cover his nose. When they arrived at a door which Mr. Melamed presumed led to the Earl's living quarters, Well'ngone opened it and motioned to Mr. Melamed to enter the room. Mr. Melamed did so, and to his surprise the door was closed behind him and he heard the sound of a key turning in the lock.

This unexpected turn of events was mildly alarming. However, he knew that thieves only rarely resorted to violence and so he was almost certain that he was not in any real danger. He therefore decided to pass the time by making a leisurely examination of the room, which was drearier than he had imagined a room could be, and he considered himself to have an excellent imagination.

As his eyes adjusted from the bright sunlight outside to the dimness of what he hoped to be only a temporary prison cell, he saw that no rays of sunlight had ever brightened the neglected space. The reason for the sun's absence was simple. There were no windows to disturb the expanse of the room's four stone walls, all of which were heavily streaked with damp and mold. If the fragrance, which was even stronger inside the room than it had been in the stairwell, was any indication, the dampness was most likely seepage from the sewer below.

He could see all this because of the light cast by half a dozen candles, which sat perched in a lopsided candelabra, which in turn sat upon the room's lone table. What he couldn't see was the purpose of his being locked up in this room. And so as he waited to see what would happen next, he wondered if he should use the opportunity to conduct a more thorough search of the room and perhaps discover a clue pertaining to the whereabouts of Simon.

Despite Mr. Melamed's assessment of the relative security of his situation, this moment in our narrative might seem to certain Readers to be a most opportune time to embark upon a spine-tingling excursion into the Gothic. However, they would be wrong. For as anyone who has ever read a novel by Mrs. Radcliffe knows, a spine-tingling search can only be conducted at midnight, preferably on a moonless night, and with one candle — not half a dozen. Furthermore, this one candle must be mysteriously extinguished just when the heroine of the story is about to discover something interesting, and if when the light is extinguished the mournful sound of a mysterious lute being played in a distant forest is suddenly heard, so much the better. Even better still is if — after the room is almost completely dark and the sound of the lute has died away — the heroine should suddenly hear the ominous sound of approaching footsteps loudly echoing in a passageway just beyond the locked door. For then the scene is complete and ready for the heroine to either collapse onto the cold stone floor in a fear-inspired faint or, if she is made of stronger stuff, collapse onto an uncomfortable chair conveniently situated next to a cold and cheerless hearth, where she may burst into tears and fall into a restless sleep until dawn.

Since none of these conditions could be met — for it was midday and not midnight; and although the room was dark and dreary, it was merely shabby and lacked the noble marks of antiquity that would entitle it to be considered an interesting ruin; and, even more seriously, Mr. Melamed was a gentleman with steady nerves and not a young lady of a more sensitive sensibility — the Narrator must disappoint those of her Readers who were hoping for the addition of a few Gothic touches to her story and, instead, request that they be content with a factual description of the mundane events which are about to transpire.

And so to continue with our narrative without further interruption, Mr. Melamed had only just finished his cursory tour of the chamber when the door was unlocked and Well'ngone entered the room.

"The Earl of Gravel Lane," Well'ngone called out with a booming voice.

Mr. Melamed turned toward the open door and saw a lad who was probably no more than fifteen or sixteen years old, despite his attempt to appear more mature, enter. The Earl, as he called himself, was a tall and skinny fellow who wore a threadbare silk coat cut in the style popular before the French Revolution. Its color, which in the past had probably been a brilliant hue, could now only be described as grime blue. Most likely, the coat had been trimmed with braids of either gold or silver thread, for Mr. Melamed noted that there were faded streaks about the pockets and collar which showed that something of value had long ago been removed. The original buttons, which would have either been made from gold or silver, or perhaps encrusted with jewels, had also long ago disappeared, for the few that still hung on the coat by plain cotton threads were made of a much baser metal.

Yet Mr. Melamed had to admit that the Earl wore his cast-off courtier's coat with aplomb, just as the dirty powdered wig stuck upon his head was worn with a certain amount of flair. The Earl didn't seem to mind that styles had changed and the day of the fop had come to an end many years earlier. One day the current age's fashionable clothing would also find its way to Gravel Lane, for styles in clothing might come and go but poverty never went out of fashion.

The Earl, who had been followed into the room by his retinue of ragged and underfed children, stopped a little way from Mr. Melamed and struck a pose. He then removed a slightly battered tin snuffbox from his coat pocket and, after snapping open the lid with his index finger, extended the snuffbox in Mr. Melamed's direction.

"Snuff, Mr. Melamed?"

Mr. Melamed normally didn't take snuff, but he considered that in this instance perhaps it was better to be polite and accept the invitation. He therefore took a pinch of the powdery substance lying inside the metal box and held it up to his nose.

"Sawdust?" he inquired.

"It's my own private blend," the Earl replied with a laugh, as he snapped the box shut without, of course, taking any "snuff" himself.

Apparently, Mr. Melamed had passed his first test, for the Earl invited him to sit down at the table and tell him what had brought him to Gravel Lane. It was an interesting question, because naturally Mr. Melamed could not openly state the real reason for his call, which was to discover the whereabouts of Simon and learn if the Earl had any connection to the theft. However, he also knew that it would be pointless to pretend that he had come to Gravel Lane to seek out the Earl's advice on some matter pertaining to the community, and so he decided to take the Earl into his confidence, although in a roundabout manner.

"It has come to my attention that a burglary has been committed at a shop in London," he began, noncommittally.

"No," replied the Earl, with a look of exaggerated alarm upon his face. "A burglary? In London? I'm in shock. Isn't that right, boys? Aren't we in shock?"

The little crowd all made a great show of shaking their heads and wringing their hands and sighing.

"I had no idea my news would cause you such distress," Mr. Melamed replied coolly. "Perhaps you are in need of some smelling salts to restore you to health?"

"Thank you, Mr. Melamed, that's very kind of you. But it's smelly enough in here as it is."

On cue, the other boys laughed. Then the Earl glanced over at Well'ngone, who immediately raised his hand and silenced the group.

"But why have you come here, Mr. Melamed? Surely you don't think that I had anything to do with this burglary. Do you?"

"Is it so obvious that you have not?"

"My line of business is picking people's pockets. Breaking into a shop requires an entirely different set of skills."

"But what if you were able to get your hands on a key to the shop? Would pinching a strongbox still require a different set of skills?"

There was a long silence, and in that silence Mr. Melamed could feel some dozen pairs of eyes upon him, none of them friendly.

"Mr. Melamed, are you aware that if I were to be convicted of the crime of stealing from a shop, I would be sentenced to hang?"

The Earl placed his chin in the palm of his hand and, smiling sweetly, gazed into Mr. Melamed's eyes. However, Mr. Melamed found that he did not feel particularly sentimental about the young man's plight. If the community had a responsibility toward the individual, the individual also had a responsibility to the community. There was such a thing as free will. Even a person forced to live in dire poverty could still be an honest man. The Earl, however, was a thief and a destroyer of souls, and he had to be dealt with as such.

On the other hand, Mr. Melamed did not intend to be the one to turn over any Jewish thief to the English courts. The Earl would eventually stumble and fall into the hands of the Bow Street Runners of his own accord. Mr. Melamed was sure of that. As for the theft from Mr. Lyon's shop, Mr. Melamed hoped to be able to resolve that matter quietly and within the community.

However, the Earl didn't have to know that, and so he replied, as he calmly returned the young man's gaze, "Yes, I am aware of that."

The two men sat in silence for several long moments. The Earl was the first to turn away. "Then search," said the Earl, with a nonchalant gesture of his hand. "And if you find the stolen goods in my home, I shall ask the court to grant you the privilege of personally escorting me to the gallows."

That response did succeed in knocking Mr. Melamed momentarily off guard. However, he quickly regained his composure and considered his next move. The strongbox would have been disposed of on the night of the theft, he reckoned, and so there was no point in looking for it. The bulk of the money, though, could still be on the premises. A person like the Earl couldn't just walk into a bank and ask to deposit a thousand guineas without raising suspicions.

On the other hand, the Earl would not have offered to let him search the place if he thought there was the slightest chance that the money would be found. So if the Earl did have the money, it had to be hidden somewhere else in the building. Therefore, Mr. Melamed would only make a fool of himself if he took the Earl's offer and searched this room. Was that the Earl's game, he wondered? To make a fool of him? Or was the Earl up to something more serious?

Then he remembered. He had come to find the child, who possibly held the key to solving the mystery.

"Actually, I don't believe you are involved," said Mr. Melamed. "I have been led to believe that the crime was committed by a child, a boy of eight or thereabouts. If you could help me locate this boy, I can guarantee that you will be amply rewarded."

The Earl of Gravel Lane suddenly stood up

and motioned to Well'ngone, who immediately snapped to attention.

"Show this man to the door, General Well'ngone," he said with an expressionless tone of voice. Then he turned a cold eye upon Mr. Melamed and said, "And as for you, sir, I advise you not to return to Gravel Lane. In this part of town, people might steal handkerchiefs, but we don't steal boys and turn them over to the gallows — and we're not fond of gentlemen who do."

Well'ngone came up to Mr. Melamed and escorted him to the door, military style. Mr. Melamed was marched up the stairs ahead of the "general," who every once in a while prodded the older man in the back with his stick, to make Mr. Melamed walk faster. This treatment, disrespectful as it was, turned out to be a blessing in disguise, for just before he reached the building's front door Mr. Melamed suddenly spied a pair of two scared eyes peering down at him from in between the spindly railings located on the floor above.

"Simon!" Mr. Melamed called out, as he bolted up the stairs.

The child, however, ran even faster. Within minutes he had reached the top floor of the building and flung open the door that led to the roof. Mr. Melamed followed him up the stairs, and he, in turn, was followed in hot pursuit by Well'ngone and the other children. Just as Mr.

Melamed reached the door to the roof, he could feel someone give a hard tug on the back of his coat. In an instant, he flung off the coat and threw it over the head of Well'ngone, who fell backward and sent the other children tumbling back down the stairs, as well. Then Mr. Melamed ran through the open door and closed it quickly behind him. Seeing that there was a latch on the outside of the door, he maneuvered the lock into place. For a few minutes, at least, he could be alone with the child. But where was he?

Mr. Melamed scanned the rooftop with worried eyes. He didn't see the child anywhere.

"Simon?" he called out.

There was no answer.

The world was strangely quiet up there, he noted, as he heard the sound of his footsteps echo against the roof's tiles. It was empty, too. But then he saw a large bin sitting at the back of the roof, and so he walked in its direction. It seemed to him that his footsteps became louder and louder with each additional step and he wondered if the child was as disturbed by the sound as he was — if Simon was still on the roof and could hear him.

When he reached the bin, he slowly bent down his head and peered inside. Peering back at him were two big eyes.

"Please, sir," he heard a small voice say from deep within the darkness, "I don't want to swing."

Chapter Ten

"**I** DON'T WANT YOU TO SWING either," Mr. Melamed replied, as he lifted Simon out of the bin. "Let's go to my home and we'll have a talk."

"I can't do that, Mr. Melamed. The Earl says I mustn't trust anyone, except him."

At that moment, Mr. Melamed saw a black bicorne hat appear at the edge of the roof's floor. The hat was followed by the person of Well'ngone, who had scaled the building's wall, a feat he had accomplished by climbing out of the window of the uppermost floor, whose ledge was not far at all from the roof. Well'ngone was quickly followed by six of his troops, all of whom were carrying large sticks and prepared for battle.

"Surrender!" Well'ngone called out, as the others formed a circle around Mr. Melamed and Simon.

Once Well'ngone was assured that his men had control of the situation, he went to unlock the door to the roof. A few moments later, the Earl, who was carrying Mr. Melamed's coat in one hand and his handkerchief in the other, sauntered outside. The sunlight was not kind to the Earl, for it showed off the pallor of his skin and the threadbare sheen of his silk coat.

"This child is a ward of the Jewish community," Mr. Melamed said to the Earl. "You have no right to detain him."

"Simon is free to go whenever he wishes," replied the Earl. "Isn't that right, Simon? Is anyone forcing you to stay with me and General Well'ngone and all your other friends?"

"No, sir."

"The same is true for you, Mr. Melamed. You, too, may leave whenever you please." The Earl then stuffed Mr. Melamed's handkerchief in his coat pocket. When he was done, he handed the coat to Mr. Melamed.

After Mr. Melamed put on his coat, he turned to the child and said, "Today, you think that the Earl is your friend. But a person who asks you to steal from your employer is not your friend, Simon. When you realize that, come to me and I'll help you in any way I can."

"But the Earl didn't ask me to steal the money, Mr. Melamed."

"Then who did?"

"No one. I wasn't the one who pinched the box. I was just the one who saw them. That's why I ran away."

"I don't understand, Simon. You saw whom?"

"The man and the boy. But it wasn't me. It was another boy. Why should I swing, if it wasn't me?"

Mr. Melamed glanced from the boy to the Earl. He noted that the Earl appeared to be calm, even somewhat disinterested in what the child had to say. Yet he wondered if the boy was telling the truth, or if the Earl had given him instructions, in the event that he was caught.

"Why don't you tell me what happened from the start, Simon?"

"Look, Squire," said Well'ngone, "we're working men. We can't stay up on this roof all day."

The Earl gave another nonchalant wave of his hand, and Well'ngone fell silent. "Speak, child," the Earl said to Simon. "You have nothing to fear from telling this man the truth. We'll protect you." The Earl then turned to Well'ngone and said, "General Well'ngone, tell your men to be at ease."

"At ease, men," Well'ngone bellowed, albeit

reluctantly, and the group settled into more comfortable positions as Simon began his tale.

The boy began by explaining that he had been feeling lonely the night before, and so he decided to climb out the orphanage's window and take a walk, which he sometimes did when his heart was troubled and he couldn't sleep. He first walked to Wormwood Street, which was not far from the orphanage, and which was the street where he had lived when his parents were still alive. After paying a short visit to his childhood home, he discovered that he was still not tired and so he decided to continue with his solitary and nocturnal exercise.

His steps led him down Bishopsgate and then to Mr. Lyon's shop on Cornhill Street. According to his testimony, he meant to do no harm. He merely stood in front of the shop and let his imagination wander to the pleasant day when he might have a shop of his own. However, he decided that if he should ever become the master of a house of clocks, he would not wait until the quarter hour or the half hour for the clocks to chime. Instead, he would set his clocks so that their pleasant music would fill his shop at every minute of the day.

While he was still imagining this happy scene, his thoughts were interrupted by what seemed to be a very real noise coming from the alleyway in back of the shop. He quietly tiptoed to the alley to see if he could discover the cause of this noise.

His quick eye saw that the door to the back room of the shop was slightly ajar, yet no light could be seen in the room.

" 'That means trouble,' I said to myself," Simon said to Mr. Melamed, "and so I decided to hide behind a barrel and wait. The next thing I knew, the door opened and a man and a boy hurried out the door. At first I thought it might be Mr. Lyon and his son, but then I asked myself, 'Now why would Mr. Lyon come to the shop at this hour with his little boy? They're both here on this earth, and so they can have their tea together any time they please. They don't have to take walks when they're lonely, like me.' "

Simon went on to explain that he decided to follow the strange man and boy, who were walking quickly in the direction of the Royal Exchange.

"Which is in the opposite direction of Gravel Lane," Well'ngone helpfully pointed out.

Mr. Melamed acknowledged with a nod of his head that he, too, knew where the Royal Exchange was located. For, after all, it is a large building filled with many shops and businesses and so surely there are few people in London who are not familiar with its location. Simon then continued with his story.

When the man and the boy came upon an open crate that was filled with rubbish, Simon saw the man toss something inside it. While the mysterious pair hurried onward, Simon stopped to investigate what had been so carelessly cast away. To his surprise, he saw that it was a key — and not just any key, for he thought it bore a striking resemblance to the key of Mr. Lyon's store.

"Do you still have the key?" asked Mr. Melamed.

Simon glanced over at the Earl of Gravel Lane. The Earl nodded his head.

"Yes, sir, I do," said Simon. He pulled out the key from his pocket and gave it to Mr. Melamed.

Mr. Melamed said nothing, but he was thinking, The third key. To Simon, he said, "What did you do next? Did you go back to Mr. Lyon's shop?"

"No, sir. You see, my heart was telling me that the man was up to no good. So if I was to go back to the shop and someone was to see me, they wouldn't believe that I was trying to do Mr. Lyon a favor and lock up his shop. They would think that I had stolen the money. So I went back to the orphanage and pretended that I had never left my bed."

"What made you believe that something had been stolen?"

"Because the next morning, when I reported for work and came into the back room, I saw Mr. Lyon on his knees and peering down into a hole in the floor. Then his face got all queer and he got up and stumbled into the front room of the shop and fainted straight away."

"But why do you believe that it was money that had been stolen?"

"I may not be an educated man like you, Mr. Melamed, but I'm not a fool. A person doesn't hide his tea things under a floorboard and then faint because he's discovered that somebody's pinched a lump of his sugar."

The other boys laughed, and this time Mr. Melamed laughed with them.

"Very well, then," said Mr. Melamed, "let us say that something of great value was taken from the shop. But I ask again, how do you know it was money? Perhaps it was something else. Perhaps there were important papers stashed underneath the floor — military secrets, for instance."

"You mean to say that Mr. Lyon is a spy?"

"No, that is not what I mean to say. I am merely asking why you are sure that it was money that was stolen, and not something else?"

Simon again glanced in the Earl's direction.

"Squire, why don't you let Simon finish with his story," said the Earl, "and then you can ask your questions."

Mr. Melamed nodded to Simon, and the boy continued. "Mr. Warburg arrived at the shop at about the same time that Mr. Lyon got sick. He told me to go fetch a doctor, and so I ran to the home of a gentleman who lives nearby. While the doctor was examining Mr. Lyon, Mr. Warburg went into the back room. I followed him and I saw him go over to the desk and look down at the hole in the floor. Then he looked over at me and gave me a queer sort of look. Mr. Warburg went back into the front room, because the doctor was calling for him, and that's when I said to myself, 'Simon, it's time for you to skiddle.'"

"To skiddle?"

"That's an expression of Mr. Muller, sir. He says that where he's from, up north, people use it to describe what happens when a jug of milk falls on the floor and the milk starts to go in every direction. It skiddles. Mr. Muller says that this is what we boys do when it's time for our lessons. We skiddle."

"I see. And so this morning you thought it best to skiddle from the shop?"

"That's right. Because if Mr. Lyon were to find out that I had in my possession the key and a guinea..."

"A guinea?" asked Mr. Melamed.

Once again, Simon glanced over at the Earl.

"You forgot that part, Simon," said the Earl. "You'd better tell Mr. Melamed everything you know."

"That's how I know it was money that was stolen, Mr. Melamed. When the man and the boy were hurrying down the alleyway, a coin dropped from the box the man was carrying. The boy bent down to get it, but the guinea had rolled away. He was going to try to find it, when the man told him not to bother and so they went on down the alley. But I knew where the coin went to, and so before I followed them I picked it up. But it wasn't me that stole it, Mr. Melamed. And I'd give it back to Mr. Lyon, except..."

The boy again glanced in the direction of the Earl.

The Earl removed a guinea from his pocket, which he showed to Mr. Melamed. "I accepted this coin as advance payment for his room and board. I have a kind heart, Squire, but unlike some people I'm not in a position to run a charitable institution."

Mr. Melamed was silent for several long moments as he considered the truth of Simon's testimony. He could see how a lonely child might take solace in visiting the place where he had known happier times. Yet it was odd that Simon would then take a stroll down to Cornhill, and odder still that he should just happen to be in the alley at the exact moment when the thieves left the shop.

"Did you see the face of either the man or the boy?" he asked Simon.

"No, sir. There was no moon and so the alley was dark."

"Yet you saw the guinea."

" 'The light of the righteous rejoices,' " said the Earl.

" 'But the lamp of the wicked shall be put out,' "

replied Mr. Melamed, completing the verse. "I can also quote from the Book of Proverbs. But that doesn't explain how Simon saw the coin."

"Not see, Squire, hear," said Well'ngone. "He heard the coin drop. And if your pockets were as empty as Simon's, you'd be able to hear a coin drop, as well."

"Very well, he heard the coin drop," said Mr. Melamed. "And, Simon, you also heard the man speak. How would you describe the man's speech? Would you say he was a gentleman or..."

"Oh, he was a gentleman, sir, for certain. The same as you and Mr. Lyon."

"And why are you so certain that he was a gentleman?"

"Because he and the boy spoke in a foreign language."

"What language did they speak?"

"I wouldn't know, sir. But it was foreign. It wasn't English and it wasn't Yiddish."

❖ ❖ ❖

AFTER HE RETURNED SIMON TO the orphanage, Mr. Melamed returned to his own home, where he had a quiet meal in the small sitting room, as he didn't like to dine alone in the larger and more formal dining room. He was glad that he had succeeded in removing the child from the Earl and his companions. And fortunately Mr. Muller had believed his story that Simon's absence from the warehouse had been a false alarm. The child had merely gotten lost, he told Mr. Muller, and no harm had been done.

Yes, Mr. Muller had believed his story. But should he believe the child's story? He wanted to. And he could see how a child who was alone in the world could have been so frightened that he ran away, even though he was innocent. If the Bow Street Runners had been on the case and discovered that a boy was involved, they wouldn't have cared too much if they picked up the wrong one — especially if that boy had in his possession a key to the shop and a guinea.

But if Simon was innocent, why had he hung on to the key? And if he had run to the Earl out of fear, why hadn't the Earl disposed of the key for him? If the Earl was using the child to steal, and they meant to steal from Mr. Lyon again, when there was a new strongbox and more money, why hadn't the Earl had Simon return the key to the desk? The child had the opportunity to do it in the morning, after Mr. Lyon became ill, and no one would have known that the key had ever been missing. Why hang on to such an incriminating piece of evidence if you don't want to hang?

Was it because the child, in his innocence, hoped that the key would serve as proof that he had told the truth about what he had seen? Or was the Earl of Gravel Lane trying to make a fool of him again?

"Will there be anything else, sir?"

Mr. Melamed's butler had entered the room and begun to clear the dishes from the table. Mr. Melamed was very tired, after his exhausting day, and he would have liked to tell his staff that they could lock up for the night. However, he knew that Mr. Lyon must be anxiously waiting to hear from him.

"Please have the carriage sent round in half an hour."

"Yes, sir."

The butler finished clearing the table and left the room, while Mr. Melamed lingered for a few more minutes over his coffee. When a drop of the dark liquid fell upon his waistcoat, he reached for his handkerchief to wipe away the spot. A soft clanging sound announced that something had dropped out of his handkerchief and fallen onto the floor.

It was a button, he soon discovered, and not an ordinary one. It was engraved with some sort of insignia, perhaps the symbol of a noble house. He supposed it must have fallen off of a servant's coat, for the servants of a duke or earl often wore coats that sported the insignia of their titled employers. And as for who had placed the button within his handkerchief, of that he had no doubt. The Earl of Gravel Lane had made a big show of stuffing his handkerchief into his coat's pocket, when they were up on the roof. But why?

Was the Earl trying to mislead him again? It seemed highly doubtful that the Earl would try to help him, since they were hardly friends. Perhaps the button was meant to throw him off the scent and keep him occupied for a day or two, while the Earl found a way to dispose of the money.

Yet there was a chance — even though it was a slight one — that the Earl was sincere in his attempt to protect Simon from the gallows. But how could a button help the child? And if it could help, why hadn't the child mentioned it earlier? Why did the Earl feel he had to convey the clue to him in such a secretive manner?

An answer to his last question soon presented itself to him. If the child had found a piece of evidence that linked a member of the nobility to the burglary, it wouldn't have saved him. There wasn't a magistrate in England who would believe his story. They would say that Simon had stolen the button, or found it in the gutter. And they would show no mercy to a street urchin who dared to accuse his betters. However, if a wealthy gentleman who was a respectable member of the community were to find the incriminating evidence, it would be a fairer fight.

Reluctantly he realized that whatever game it

was that the Earl was playing, he had been pulled into it. He could easily discover if the button belonged to one of Lord Grenville's servants by making a visit to the button's maker, whose mark was on the button's back. This he would do on the morrow. Tonight, though, he had other work to do. For even though he hoped that Mr. Lyon was holding up well under the pressure, his suspicions told him that the man might need some encouragement. He therefore wrapped the button in his handkerchief, stuffed the two objects into a drawer, and went to get his hat.

Chapter Eleven

PERL, THE FAMILY'S MAID, ANSWERED the front door of the Lyons' home. Mr. Melamed was about to speak when the sound of a child's plaintive cry stopped him. Then the door to the drawing room suddenly opened and a small boy, dressed in a nightshirt and slippers, darted out the door and, still wailing, raced up the stairs.

"Joshua! You get into bed right now!" shouted a young lady, as she chased the child up the stairs. (Reader, I am embarrassed to admit it, but this young lady was I.) "And if you sneak into the drawing room again and listen to other people's private conversations, I'll give you another spanking."

Through the still open door, Mr. Melamed could hear the sound of a woman sobbing. He was beginning to wonder if he should postpone his call until the next day, when Mr. Lyon exited the room and called up to his daughter, "Rebecca, please, no more spanking. And Joshua, you do as your sister says and go to bed."

As Mr. Lyon turned to go back into the room, he spotted Mr. Melamed standing in the vestibule, and said, "Mr. Melamed? How kind of you to call. Perl, please bring tea to the drawing room."

Perl curtsied and left. Mr. Melamed followed Mr. Lyon into the drawing room. From the sobbing figure of Mrs. Lyon and the pale face of the family's eldest daughter, Hannah, he understood that they knew everything.

"I tried not to say anything, Mr. Melamed, truly I tried. And the little ones don't know. But I couldn't continue to keep such a terrible secret from my dear wife, or from Hannah and Rebecca. They know me too well. While they were discussing the wedding, I broke down into tears. Of course, they guessed that something was wrong."

"Do you have any news for us, Mr. Melamed?" asked Mrs. Lyon, through her sobs. "Even a crumb? Anything to sustain us during this difficult time?"

Rebecca Lyon re-entered the room at that moment, and she took a seat beside her elder sister. Her younger sisters were upstairs, fast asleep, and she hoped that Joshua would follow their excellent example, because she wanted to hear what Mr. Melamed had to say.

"Shall we let Mr. Melamed sit down first, my dear?" Mr. Lyon said to his wife.

Mr. Melamed took a seat and looked around at the little circle of expectant faces, not knowing what to say. But as he looked at their faces, he knew that Mrs. Lyon was right. He did have to give them something, even if it was just a crumb of hope, and so he said, "I intend to write a letter to Abraham Goldsmid."

"The financier?" asked Mr. Lyon.

"Yes. I shan't mention any names, because as I mentioned before, it is most important that news of your financial ruin does not reach your business creditors. However, I shall inform Mr. Goldsmid that a certain businessman needs a free loan to keep his business afloat. I am certain that we will be able to come to an agreement. You, Mr. Lyon, will need to tell me what sum to request and give me an idea of how long it will take you to pay it back."

"I shall attend to the matter this evening."

"As for the marriage of your daughter to David Goldsmith, I am confident that everything can be worked out. I know of someone who would be happy to take on the *mitzvah* of paying all the expenses for the wedding. And as for the rooms on

Bury Street, the young couple may live there for as long as they like. We will keep a record, and you will pay me when you are able to."

"Mr. Melamed, this is all too good of you!" Mrs. Lyon exclaimed, dabbing at her eyes with her handkerchief. "You are like an angel sent to us from Heaven. Is he not exactly like an angel, dear Hannah?"

Hannah was silent. Her own handkerchief was being so tightly grasped by her hands that her knuckles were quite white from the pressure. Yet they were not as white as her down-turned face, which appeared to be totally devoid of color. Although it was possible to assume that Hannah could not speak because she was overwhelmed with relief and gratitude, Rebecca suspected that her sister's reticence was due to a very different and more worrisome cause. However, this was neither the time nor the place to give voice to her suspicions.

Attention was diverted from Hannah by the appearance of Perl, who had knocked and brought in the tea things. The little group was silent while the tea and plate of cakes were passed around.

"That will be all, Perl," said Mrs. Lyon.

"Yes, ma'am." Perl made a little curtsy. But before she left the room, she gave a parting glance at Hannah, who had declined both the tea and the cakes.

When the door to the drawing room was closed

once again, Mr. Lyon turned to Mr. Melamed and asked, "But what about the thief? Have you made any progress with discovering his identity?"

"Only a little, but I am still confident of finding the person who stole the money. In fact, I have reason to believe that the deed might have been done by two people."

"Two people?" Mr. Lyon asked with surprise.

"A man and a child."

"I knew it!"

Mr. Melamed, who had been in the process of stirring his tea, gave a start. He had not expected such an extreme reaction and he looked to see who had spoken.

"I said as much, Mr. Lyon. Did I not say the same thing to your father, girls?"

"Mrs. Lyon, please let Mr. Melamed continue to speak," said Mr. Lyon, before his daughters could reply.

"I'm afraid I don't understand," said Mr. Melamed. "Has some new information come to light that I should know about?"

"No," Mr. Lyon replied, quite firmly. "My wife believes that she knows the identity of the thief, but it is only a little fantasy that she has dreamed up."

"The friendship between Mr. Oppenheim and that messenger boy of yours is not something I dreamed up, Samuel," Mrs. Lyon protested. "You said yourself that when Mr. Oppenheim left for Manchester the child was quite beside himself with grief."

"Is this true, Mr. Lyon?" asked Mr. Melamed. "Were they really such good friends?"

"They were two people from the same part of Bohemia who found themselves alone in London, and so Mr. Oppenheim took a brotherly interest in Simon. When there were no customers in the shop to wait upon, he used to teach Simon a little Torah. When Simon learned well, Mr. Oppenheim would give the child a piece of cake or an apple, and so of course the child was fond of his teacher. I can't see what was wrong in that, or why Mrs. Lyon thinks this has something to do with the burglary."

"I have explained my reasoning to you three times," Mrs. Lyon replied. Then she turned to their guest and said, "I ask you, Mr. Melamed, as an impartial observer, do you not think it strange that Mr. Oppenheim came to London on the very day the theft was committed? What was his business here? Why would he not speak with my husband?"

Mr. Melamed did not reply, because he had the very same questions.

"I told you, Mrs. Lyon, he was pressed for time," said Mr. Lyon. "I am sure he will call upon us before he returns to Manchester."

"I asked Mr. Melamed for his opinion, Mr. Lyon," replied Mrs. Lyon.

All eyes turned to Mr. Melamed, who said, quietly, "Mr. Oppenheim has already returned to Manchester. I spoke to his landlady this afternoon."

"There, you see!" Mrs. Lyon exclaimed. "Your goodness has blinded you to the truth, Mr. Lyon. But my eyes are wide open, and in my opinion Mr. Oppenheim had it all worked out with that child. The boy knew that Mr. Oppenheim was coming to London and he removed the key from your desk when no one was looking. Then, after you and Mr. Warburg had gone home for the night, he unlocked the door for Mr. Oppenheim and they stole the strongbox. Mr. Oppenheim and the boy then returned to Manchester, with your one thousand guineas."

"I refuse to listen to any more of your slanderous talk, Mrs. Lyon," said Mr. Lyon, becoming quite heated. "Jacob was like a son to me. He would not do anything to harm me. I know it."

Mr. Lyon took out his handkerchief and wiped his brow. He then turned to Mr. Melamed and said, "I know that Mrs. Lyon wishes to help, but she was not as closely acquainted with Mr. Oppenheim as I was, and so she was not able to form an accurate picture of his character. I, however, am in a better position to judge the young man and so I must again request that you strike the name of Mr. Oppenheim from your list of suspects."

Mrs. Lyon began to jab at the lumps of sugar in the sugar bowl quite vigorously, but she did not say another word. Mr. Lyon therefore said, "But we haven't let you speak, Mr. Melamed. Perhaps you have discovered the whereabouts of the third key? Perhaps you have developed a theory of your own?"

Mr. Melamed began to feel slightly sick to his stomach. "Simon is still in London, Mrs. Lyon," he said, choosing his words carefully. "He did not go to Manchester."

"Aha!" exclaimed Mr. Lyon. "Well done, Mr. Melamed. I knew the boy had nothing to do with any of this. And when you find the key..."

"I did find the third key."

"You did? Where?"

"In Simon's pocket."

Mr. Lyon looked at Mr. Melamed, unable to say a word.

"I am going to make a trip to Manchester, Mr. Lyon. I think you should join me."

❖ ❖ ❖

THAT NIGHT, NEITHER HANNAH NOR Rebecca could sleep. Although Hannah tried to pretend that she was not crying, and Rebecca tried to pretend that she was not crying, before long the two sisters were sobbing in each other's arms.

"Don't cry, Hannah, please," said Rebecca.

"Everything is going to be fine. Didn't you hear what Mr. Melamed said? He's going to take care of us."

"Oh, yes, he's going to care of us, just like he takes care of the children in the orphanage, just like he takes care of all his charity cases. He'll buy us the food we eat, and the clothes we wear, and we shall be paupers, totally dependent upon the kindness of others."

"But only for a little while, until Papa can recover his money."

"It took Papa all his life to make his fortune. He won't make another one so quickly."

"Then we shall learn how to live simpler lives. I shall eat only one slice of toast in the morning, and not two. And I shall not ask Perl to make a fire in our room unless it's very, very cold. But you will still be able to marry Mr. Goldsmith, and that's what is important."

"No, I cannot."

"Why not? Mr. Melamed said..."

"Mr. Melamed! Mr. Melamed said many things. But Mr. Melamed forgot to take into account one thing that is of utmost importance."

Rebecca stared at her sister. She had never heard Hannah speak in such a harsh tone of voice, and she was afraid to see this change in her sister. "What, Hannah? What did Mr. Melamed forget?"

"He forgot to ask if Miss Hannah Lyon, pauper, wishes to receive charity. For if he had asked Miss Hannah Lyon, pauper, if she wished to receive charity, she would have told him, 'No, sir, she does not.'"

"But the Goldsmiths don't need to know that someone else is going to pay for the wedding, or that Mr. Goldsmid is going to give Papa a loan."

"They will find out."

"Even if they do, surely it won't matter."

"Surely it will. How would you feel, Rebecca, if you discovered, after your wedding, that your husband had lied to you? That he had told you that he was a wealthy man, when he knew all along that he was really a pauper?"

"I suppose I should be very hurt."

"And rightfully so. And how would you like living in a home where your husband and in-laws looked down upon you, because you come from a poor family — and not an honest poor family, but a family that stooped to trickery to marry off their penniless daughter to a wealthy man's son?"

"I suppose I shouldn't like that, either. But, Hannah, the Goldsmiths are good people. They wouldn't look down upon you just because you are poor. They would see all your good qualities, and value you for that."

"If they had entered into the marriage agreement knowing my true financial state, perhaps you are right, although I do doubt it, Rebecca. There are other young ladies, you know."

Rebecca did know, and this was why she suddenly thought of Brighton and all the young ladies who were there. She shivered as she contemplated the thought of one of them making a *shidduch* with the very eligible and suddenly available Mr. Goldsmith. However, her disturbing thoughts were distracted by the sight of Hannah reaching for her shawl and then lighting the candle that stood beside her bed. As Hannah carried the candle over to the writing table and sat down, Rebecca asked, "Hannah, what are you doing?"

"I am going to write Mr. Goldsmith a letter. I shall tell him that I wish to break off the engagement."

"You can't!"

"I must."

"No, Hannah, we must give Mr. Melamed a chance. Perhaps he will find the thief."

"Perhaps he will. But even if he finds the thief, he won't find the rest of Father's money. We shall still be poor."

"But everything can change in a blink of an eye. Don't you believe that?"

"Of course, I do."

"Then why not wait? You don't have to write to **Mr. Goldsmith now. At least wait until he returns from Brighton.**"

A knock at the door startled them both. Hannah called out, "Who is it?"

"It's me, Miss Hannah. It's Perl," a voice whispered from the other side of the door.

"Come in," said Hannah, and Perl entered the room.

"I'm sorry to disturb you, Miss Hannah, and I hope you won't think it impertinent of me, coming to your room like this."

"Of course not, Perl. Is something wrong?"

"Well, there is something wrong, isn't there? I didn't mean to, but I couldn't help but overhear a little bit of what was being discussed in the drawing room this evening. I talked it over with my mother and father, and we decided that we would like to give you this, Miss Hannah, to help pay for your wedding. It isn't much, but we did want to help."

Perl took out a handkerchief from the pocket of her apron. The handkerchief had been tied tightly at the top, so that it made a little pouch that could hold a small amount of coins.

"Please take it, Miss Hannah."

Hannah stared at the white handkerchief. Tears began to form in her eyes. "Thank you very much, Perl. And please thank your parents. I'm very touched by your kindness, but I can't take your money. I can't."

Hannah laid her head upon the writing table and began to weep. Perl watched in silence for a few moments, and then she turned to Rebecca and said, "Everything has changed, hasn't it?"

Rebecca slowly nodded her head. "Yes, it has."

✦ ✦ ✦

IN A STREET NOT TOO far away from Devonshire Square, another candle was burning. The candle belonged to Mr. Melamed, who also could not sleep. He stood at the open window in his library, staring up at the starry sky.

As he gazed at the celestial show taking place above him, he could not help but note the contrast between the harmonious order of the cosmos and the disorder that seemed to be the hallmark of this troubled little world below. The stars, despite there being millions of them, did not push or quarrel. No star ever had a thought to steal the light of another so that it could shine more brightly. There were boundaries, and the stars accepted these boundaries. And unlike humans, they knew that a world that did not respect the boundaries set up by the Creator was a world that set itself up to know only chaos and destruction. It would never know the sublime gifts of harmony and peace.

It was remarkable what one criminal act could do, he realized, as he turned his gaze away from the night sky and looked down upon the letter in his hand, which he had started to write but had not yet finished. An act of theft, such as the one that had taken place in Mr. Lyon's shop, was an act that unleashed into the world the destroying forces of chaos. Lives that had been going forward to an orderly end were suddenly thrown off course and sent spinning into an unknown direction. Hannah Lyon and David Goldsmith, for instance, who should have built a home together, might now be thrown apart; that home might never be built. The home built by Hannah's parents, which had previously been a haven of harmony and tranquility, was now filled with arguments and quarrels. And then there was Simon. Until a few days ago, the child was on the path of becoming an honest young man, with a future in Mr. Lyon's warehouse. Tonight, his future seemed to lead to the gallows.

Did the thief, whoever he was, have any idea of all the harm he had done? Mr. Melamed wondered. Was he at all aware of all that he had destroyed? Or had he never looked up at the night sky and been filled with a sense of awe and wonder at the sublime harmony of the universe, and taken its cosmic lessons to heart?

As he contemplated these matters, Mr. Melamed again felt overwhelmed by the responsibility he had taken on. He still hoped that he would be able to **repair some of the damage done by the thief, and so returned his attention to the letter in his hand.**

The letter was not to his eldest daughter who lived on the Continent, where her husband was engaged in business. Instead, the letter was addressed to the leader of a Chassidic sect that his son-in-law and daughter had become involved with. Supposedly, this Rebbe of theirs was a miracle worker, and Mr. Melamed's daughter often wrote him about the miraculous salvations that the Rebbe brought about for his followers.

Mr. Melamed wasn't entirely sure that he approved of these Chassidic Rebbes, and he always read his daughter's letters with a certain amount of skepticism. However, on this evening he needed a salvation of his own. He needed to discover the identity of the thief and restore harmony to his little world. And so he had decided to write to this Rebbe and ask for his blessing and assistance.

Since charity was a powerful remedy for all things, Mr. Melamed slipped inside the letter a bill of exchange, which the Rebbe could exchange for cash to distribute to the poor. It was preferable to distribute charity secretly, he knew. That way the poor people didn't know where the money came from. It also allowed them to retain their dignity.

He had erred in openly revealing his charitable plans to Mr. and Mrs. Lyon and their daughters. He knew that, too. He hadn't planned on doing it. If Mr. Lyon wished to reveal his financial ruin to his family, that was his choice. But Mr. Melamed should have insisted upon speaking with Mr. Lyon privately. His only excuse was that when he saw Mrs. Lyon's distraught state, he had wanted to offer some immediate assistance. It had been a mistake, though, and he shouldn't have allowed his feelings of sympathy to overwhelm his judgment.

But he had, and now the daughter despised him. He understood her feelings, and if he had been in her position he probably would have felt the same way. Still, he hoped she wouldn't do something foolish, such as contact the Goldsmith family and tell them what had happened. There was still hope. They had to believe that.

Mr. Melamed looked down at his letter. He had only gotten as far as the salutation. He had never written to a Rebbe before, and so he wasn't sure what to say. He therefore decided to be brief, and this was what he wrote: "A certain Jewish shop owner in London has lost his fortune. If the Rebbe could help restore this man's fortune to him, so that the family shall not be reduced to relying upon charity, we should all be very much obliged."

After folding the letter, Mr. Melamed removed a stick of sealing wax from his desk drawer and held the wax above the flame of a candle. When the wax started to melt, he removed it from the flame and held it over the fold of the heavy piece of paper. As the colored wax dripped down upon the paper, he searched through the drawer for his seal, but for some strange reason he couldn't find it.

The melted wax was starting to harden. It would not be a catastrophe if the letter was not stamped with a seal, although such a thing usually wasn't done, at least not by a gentleman. Then Mr. Melamed suddenly remembered the silver button with the insignia imprinted on it, and it occurred to him that the button could be used instead, since the Rebbe would never know that this was not Mr. Melamed's personal seal. He therefore took the letter to the sitting room, where the button was still stored in a drawer.

He was able to stamp the button into the wax just in time. The letter was properly sealed. He would have one of his servants post it in the morning.

The clock struck one, reminding him that it was time for him to go to bed, which he could do with a clear conscience. He was doing his best. Now it was up to Hashem.

Chapter Twelve

THE NEXT DAY, HANNAH'S LETTER was placed on the mail coach to Brighton, while Mr. Melamed's letter began its long journey to the Continent. Having disposed of his letter, Mr. Melamed decided to make an early morning visit to the home of Isaac Warburg. It was surprising that Mrs. Lyon was so sure the culprit was the former assistant, when the present assistant was the one who had the most opportunity. Why was he the only one who suspected Mr. Warburg, he wondered?

The Warburg family lived on Harrow Street, close to Petticoat Lane, in a building so old and shabby that it looked like it had never been new. Yet when Mr. Melamed reached the top floor, where the Warburgs' rooms were located, he saw that the hall was swept and the door had been freshly painted.

Mr. Melamed stood outside the door for a few moments and listened. It usually wasn't difficult to recognize the homes that suffered from distressing economic problems — the kind of problems that could tempt an otherwise honest man to steal. Shouting, strong language, and tears were the usual telltale signs, but he heard none of them.

Mr. Warburg answered his knock, and he was more than a little surprised to see Mr. Melamed standing in the hallway. "Please come in," he said. "How can I help you, Mr. Melamed?"

Mr. Melamed accepted the invitation to enter, even as he said, "Forgive me for disturbing you, Mr. Warburg. Actually, I was looking for a family recently arrived from Poland. I must have mistaken the address. Perhaps they live on a different floor."

"I am not familiar with all the neighbors. I will ask my wife."

While Mr. Warburg spoke to his wife in German, Mr. Melamed quickly looked around the room. It was small, but very clean and very tidy. In addition to Mr. and Mrs. Warburg, there was an older woman sitting by the window. She was engaged in some sort of beadwork, while she gently rocked a wooden cradle with her foot.

Mr. Melamed noted that the blanket that covered the infant was freshly laundered, as were the lacework curtains on the window and the embroidered tablecloth on the small round dining table. The furniture in the room was obviously secondhand, but it had been dusted recently and it was clean. In the corner was a table where a pair of tall silver candlesticks sat. They were simple candlesticks, but they gleamed in the morning sunlight. He had to admit that the scene was the very picture of simple domestic peace.

"My wife is not familiar with this new family," said Mr. Warburg, after he returned to Mr. Melamed's side. "But my mother-in-law would like to show you something."

Mr. Warburg said a few words to the older woman, again in German, and she left the room. But she quickly returned, holding a beaded reticule in her hand, which she showed to Mr. Melamed.

"My mother-in-law has found employment making these purses for a shop in Mayfair," explained Mr. Warburg.

"In Mayfair?" said Mr. Melamed. "That's very impressive."

"And very helpful. We are proud of the fact that we do not need to ask for help from the synagogue's charity fund."

"May Hashem continue to bless you with prosperity."

"Amen." Mr. Warburg then escorted Mr. Melamed to the door. When they were back in the hallway, Mr. Warburg said, "I didn't take the money, Mr. Melamed. Yes, I know that this is why you are here."

"Did you see anything suspicious yesterday morning?"

"The floorboard that had been flung to the side. The hole in the floor. These things I saw."

"You knew that this was where Mr. Lyon hid the strongbox?"

"One can guess."

"Was there anything else that you saw that was suspicious?"

"Do you ask only about yesterday morning?"

"No."

"Sometimes Mr. Lyon would leave his account book sitting on his desk unattended. The messenger boy would sometimes look at it."

"Simon? Why would he do that?"

"I don't know."

"But you have your suspicions?"

"The account book does have the names and addresses of Mr. Lyon's wealthy clients. Also, Mr. Lyon would sometimes make a notation of who was still in London and who had gone to Brighton or the country. Such information could be quite useful for a thief. Of course, I am not accusing the boy of doing anything wrong. But he does have some friends who are, shall we say, less than desirable."

"Thank you, Mr. Warburg. You have been quite illuminating."

"It is my pleasure to be of help."

Mr. Melamed turned to go, and Mr. Warburg re-entered his home and shut the door. When Mr. Melamed reached the landing of the floor below, he stopped. He waited to hear if there were any sounds of discord emanating from the Warburgs' rooms, but all was quiet.

Even though he had no evidence to the contrary, Mr. Melamed still wasn't convinced that Mr. Warburg was innocent. Mr. Warburg had been much too quick to cast aspersions on an orphaned child, for his taste. On the other hand, he had never been in Mr. Warburg's position. Because Mr. Warburg was a new arrival to London, perhaps he felt that his position was so precarious that he had to do anything to protect his integrity, including deflect suspicion from himself by casting it upon someone who was even more vulnerable.

One thing he had learned, though, was that Mr. Warburg was not in collaboration with Simon. If Simon had told the truth about there being two people — a man and a boy — and Mr. Warburg was the man, then the identity of the boy was still unknown. That would let Simon off the hook.

Unfortunately, though, he had no proof that Mr. Warburg was the thief. He only had his suspicions. And so that left Simon still very much under suspicion, to his distress.

These thoughts brought Mr. Melamed to his next stop, which was to arrange for a coach to take him and Mr. Lyon to Manchester after Shabbos. It was a long journey — it would take at least eighteen hours each way — and so it was important to hire a comfortable coach suitable for such travel, as well as fast horses. Once the travel arrangements had been made, Mr. Melamed returned to his home to retrieve the button, which had been cleaned of its sealing wax. The cleaning had also helped to more clearly reveal the mark of the button's manufacturer. And so after a light luncheon, Mr. Melamed went straight to the Strand, where the shop of Firmin & Westall, buttonmakers, was located.

"Yes, sir, this is one of our buttons," Mr. Firmin, or perhaps it was Mr. Westall, informed him.

"Can you tell me who the button belongs to?" asked Mr. Melamed. "I would like to return it to its owner. It is silver, I believe."

The button manufacturer gave Mr. Melemed a look that fairly dripped with disdain. "Lord Grenville will hardly miss one button."

◆ ◆ ◆

"I HAVE A KEY, A guinea, and a button," said Mr. Melamed, as he laid the three objects on his table at Baer's Coffee House. While Simon had been happy to rid himself of the key, the Earl of Gravel Lane had been less enthused about handing over the guinea. However, he had been persuaded. The button, of course, had been a gift.

Mr. Baer studied the three objects closely. Then he sighed and said, "It doesn't make sense."

"What doesn't?"

"That all three things should drop."

"Too much of a coincidence?"

"Yes."

"So what's your theory, Asher?"

"I say that the button fell off when Lord Grenville's servants were moving the clock through the door. Samuel said it was a tight squeeze, didn't he?"

"Yes, he did."

"So the boy could have found the button during the day."

"Before he delivered the note to the warehouse?"

"That's right. Or one of the Earl's boys could have found it, when they happened to pass through the alley."

"Then Simon wouldn't have known anything about it."

"That's right."

Mr. Melamed was silent for a moment. Then he

said, "If your theory is correct, Percy Grenville had nothing to do with the theft." Mr. Melamed moved the button over to the side of the table. He then asked, "What do you make of Warburg's comment?"

"About the boy reading the account book?"

"Yes."

"I don't know."

"But you don't like it?"

"No." Mr. Baer paused. "The boy didn't have to be passing on the information to the Earl, though."

"Who else would be interested?"

"A competitor."

"Someone who wanted to steal Mr. Lyon's customers?"

"The good ones," Mr. Baer said with a laugh. "The ones who don't pay, anyone can have."

"Do you think this competitor might have paid Simon a guinea for the information?"

"He might have." Mr. Baer looked at Mr. Melamed and his jaw dropped open. "Are you thinking what I'm thinking?"

"Perhaps. What are you thinking?"

"That the boy's story was a lie, or at least the part about finding the guinea was."

"Perhaps." Mr. Melamed pushed the guinea to the other side of the table. "That leaves the key."

The two men stared at the key.

"This is tougher than a piece of meat that hasn't

been properly cooked," said Mr. Baer with a sad shake of his head.

"One mouse, or two?" Mr. Melamed murmured softly.

"What?"

"It's a problem from the Talmud. Something that Rava asked."

The two men continued to stare at the key. Then Mr. Melamed said, "It seems to me that if we take away both the button and the guinea and leave only the key, then we are left with nothing."

"How do you mean?"

"Let's say that Simon had the key and the strongbox and he opened the door. Where did he go? What did he do with the money?"

"He gave it to the Earl of Gravel Lane?"

"No. If the Earl had the money, he wouldn't have let Simon talk. He would have kept the boy locked up somewhere until the danger of being discovered had passed."

"So who did he give it to?"

"He either gave it to the guinea or the button."

"If he gave the money to Percy Grenville, you're stuck, aren't you? Isn't Lord Grenville on the side of the Reformers? The emancipation of the Jews, and all that? You don't want to do anything that would turn him against us."

"It's true that this will require some delicacy. But if Lord Grenville is an honorable man, he would surely want to know that his son is breaking into shops and stealing money."

"I see where you're leading to. A person might even say that you'd be doing Lord Grenville a favor by your letting him know what his son has gotten up to, before he tries a bigger heist and gets his name into all the scandal sheets."

"Perhaps Lord Grenville might look upon it as a favor. But it would be better for the community if the thief wasn't Percy Grenville." Mr. Melamed looked over to the door, which had just opened. "You've got a customer."

Asher looked over his shoulder to see who had come into the coffee house. He nodded to the man, and then he lowered his voice and said, "And what if it isn't Lord Button? Do you know who Mr. Guinea might be?"

Mr. Melamed knew that Mr. Baer would not be pleased to hear that Mr. Oppenheim was a prime suspect. And so as he scooped up the three objects and put them into his pocket, he replied, noncommittally, "I have my suspicions."

✦ ✦ ✦

MR. ARTHUR POWELL, THE YOUNGEST son of Lord James Powell, was at home when Mr. Melamed called. Mr. Melamed was ushered into the library, where he found Mr. Powell studying a recently purchased map of North America.

"Look at all this land, Melamed. If we could buy up even a small part of this Louisiana Purchase territory, we would be richer than..."

Mr. Powell did not finish his sentence, and so Mr. Melamed finished it for him. "Your older brother?"

Mr. Powell smiled. His father had owned vast estates in northern England, but his older brother had inherited them all. Since he received only a small yearly income from the estates, Mr. Powell had done what younger sons had done for generations before him: Created his own wealth. This he had accomplished by successfully speculating in land with Mr. Melamed.

The Powell family had a business connection with the Melamed family that went back to Solomon Melamed, Mr. Melamed's great-great-great-grandfather, who had left his native Prague in the 1670s and arrived in London in time to take part in the rebuilding of that city after the Great Fire in 1666. The elder Mr. Melamed had come to England with only an uncanny ability to spot a good piece of property when he saw one. The fact that he had no money was only a mild obstacle, since a first-generation Jewish immigrant wasn't allowed to purchase property in any event. However, circumstances brought him into contact with the Powell family, who had both money and an impeccable non-Jewish lineage, and a mutually beneficial partnership was established.

Over time, the Melamed family also became quite wealthy. And even though subsequent, native-born generations of the family were able to purchase property under English law, it was still sometimes useful to buy land in partnership with the Powells. Some impoverished noblemen preferred to sell their estates to a member of their own class, and not to a Jew.

Recently, the partnership between the two families had led to some successful ventures in the former American colonies. That was why Mr. Melamed's younger daughter had moved to New York with her husband. Someone needed to manage their properties. However, Mr. Melamed's mind was not on North America at the moment, and so he considered how he could steer the conversation round to events closer to home.

"Is your son still with the army on the Spanish peninsula?" asked Mr. Melamed.

"He'd better be. It cost me a fortune to purchase that commission for him. But I consider it to be money well spent. At least in the army he won't be able to run up huge gambling debts, like he did in London. You're lucky you had only daughters, Melamed."

"Yes, gambling seems to be the curse of our generation. Your son was friendly with Mr. Percy

Grenville, wasn't he?"

"The son of Lord Grenville? Why do you ask?"

Mr. Melamed took the hint. Arthur Powell was a friend, but Arthur Powell was also a member of the English aristocracy. His first loyalty was to his own class. He wouldn't tolerate criticism of the nobility by an outsider. Mr. Melamed decided to come straight to the point.

"Is Lord Grenville the sort of person who would prefer to avoid a family scandal being made public?" asked Mr. Melamed.

"I think so."

"Then I will be frank with you. His son, Mr. Percy Grenville, may have been involved in some unsavory business. I am hoping he was not, for Lord Grenville's sake. But is there a way that you could discover something about Mr. Grenville's activities of the last several days?"

"Where he was and what he did? That sort of thing?"

"And what he bought and how much he spent."

"I don't know. He's a young man. We don't have the same friends."

"But you do go to some of the same places? The same clubs, for example?"

"I did see him at Tattersall's the other day."

"He was buying horses?"

"He was looking at a pair of greys. Whether he bought them or not, I don't know. But why should it matter if he spent a few hundred pounds on horses? That's nothing in the social circle that young men like Mr. Grenville travel in."

"I agree that spending the money is unimportant. But what about stealing it?"

"I think I'm beginning to understand."

Chapter Thirteen

ON THE FOLLOWING SUNDAY EVENING, Mr. Melamed and Mr. Lyon set off for Manchester. "I am sorry to put you to so much trouble and expense," Mr. Lyon said, as they settled themselves into the carriage. "I am sure it will be a wasted journey."

"If we find out the truth, it will not be wasted," Mr. Melamed replied.

Mr. Lyon glanced out the carriage window. He saw his daughter Rebecca standing at the sitting room window. He waved to her, and she waved back. Then he said to Mr. Melamed, "Hannah wrote to the Goldsmiths."

"I thought she might. Have you received a reply?"

"No, not yet."

Then the driver cracked his whip and the horses set off. After the carriage and its occupants left London behind, the urban setting was quickly replaced by a rural one, and this change of scene should have provided the Narrator of this *megillah* with an excellent opportunity to make an excursion of her own into the picturesque. For what could be more natural, as the carriage lumbered down the road for eighteen long hours, than to describe the pleasantly rolling hills and the velvety green valleys; the shadowy glens of majestic trees and the ambling paths of refreshing streams; the chattering birds that frolicked overhead and the colorful flowers that bobbed their heads below; or the charming country villages coyly tucked behind a bend in the road and the amusingly rustic peasants discovered at their evening repose? What sweeping vistas to exclaim over! What lofty sentiments to indulge in! What Author worthy of the name would not have seized upon the opportunity to describe, in sublime detail, the ever-changing landscapes that surely must have been found in abundance on the winding road that led from busy and prosperous London to Manchester, her sister city in the north?

But, alas, the Narrator of this tale has never traveled further north than Oxford Street, and all that she knows of trees are that their trunks are brown and their leaves are green. Her knowledge of birds and streams is also of the most limited kind. And so, since she is not equipped to give an accurate account of the journey, she will give none at all.

Unfortunately, the occupants of the carriage similarly must decline. Mr. Melamed insists that he slept most of the way, and so he saw neither glen nor dale, picturesque or otherwise. Mr. Lyon recalls that he was so preoccupied with trying to find a comfortable position in the carriage — for he was not used to such springy travel — that he did not look out the window more than once or twice, and then all he saw was a world cloaked in darkness.

Therefore, the Reader must be content with this: They set out, they traveled all night, and they arrived safely in Manchester the next day.

✦ ✦ ✦

WHILE THE CARRIAGE CONTAINING MR. Lyon and Mr. Melamed was traveling north, Hannah's letter, which had arrived in Brighton a few days earlier, had traveled from the hand of Mr. David Goldsmith to his desk drawer and then back to his hand many times, before the letter finally reached the hand of his father. For although the young Mr. Goldsmith received the letter before Shabbos, he had been so perplexed by its contents that he hadn't wanted to mention it to his parents immediately. His hope had been that the refreshing repose of the Sabbath day would settle his troubled thoughts and enable him to read the distressing words with new eyes. However, the letter remained as disturbing after Shabbos as before.

On Monday afternoon, at a quiet moment in their Brighton shop, he decided to show the letter to his father. Mr. Mayer Goldsmith took out his spectacles and began to read. While he was still reading, a few fashionable young men entered the jewelry shop. Mr. David Goldsmith waited upon them, so that his father could finish reading the letter undisturbed.

Mr. David Goldsmith was slightly acquainted with the young men, and he knew them to be customers who thought that "credit" was the English word for gratis. He therefore did not exert himself to show them the bejeweled snuffboxes that they were admiring. However, there was another reason that he did not wish to detain the group any longer than necessary: The young men were rude.

One of the young men had brought with him his little page, who was dressed in a suit of pale blue livery and who wore a snow-white powdered wig. The child appeared to be no more than five or six years old, and if his nut-colored skin and lilting voice was any indication, he had been born in the West Indies. Despite his young age and station in life, the child had a saucy tongue, which he showed off by insulting the wares in the Goldsmiths' shop.

Since the fashionable young men laughed at the child's antics, it appeared that the boy had learned to speak disrespectfully from them.

"Ignore them," Mr. Mayer Goldsmith whispered to his son under his breath, as he placed his spectacles and the letter on the counter. Then, while still speaking in a low voice, he added, "What do you make of this letter, David?"

"I don't know. I almost don't believe that it is real."

"But if Miss Lyon did not write this letter, who did? And why?"

"Perhaps our family has an enemy who wishes to see the engagement broken off."

"On the other hand, we must consider the possibility that what is written here is true."

"How could such a thing have happened to Mr. Lyon?"

"I don't know. But we must make inquiries. We must get to the bottom of this."

Mr. Goldsmith, senior, noticed that one of the fashionable young men was standing near the counter and seemed to be listening to his conversation with his son with more than a little interest. "May I help you, sir?" he asked.

"No, I've changed my mind," Mr. Percy Grenville replied.

Mr. Grenville joined his friends, who were already standing near the door. "*Allez! Allez!*" he said to his page, and then the group departed.

Chapter Fourteen

W HEN MR. LYON AND MR. Melamed
arrived in Manchester, their first concern
was to find a comfortable inn run by good Jewish
folk, where they could remove the dust from their
clothes and partake of a quiet meal while seated at
a table and chair that did not bounce up and down.
After having refreshed themselves accordingly, Mr.
Melamed was anxious to proceed immediately to
the shop of Mr. Oppenheim. He therefore inquired
of the inn's owner if he was familiar with such an
establishment.

"It's down the street and to your right," the
innkeeper replied. "It's a tiny place, but it is right

next door to the draper's shop and so you won't miss it."

Mr. Melamed paid the bill. Then he returned to the table, where Mr. Lyon was still sitting.

"We should be going."

"What shall I say?" asked Mr. Lyon. "How can I present the question to him without insulting him? It is a terrible thing, you know, to accuse an innocent man of a crime that he has not committed."

"If you prefer, I will speak to him."

"No. I must be the one to do it. I only hope that the True Judge will give me the right words for performing this most unpleasant task."

As the innkeeper's directions were quite clear and the Jewish section of Manchester was quite small, the two men were standing inside the little shop of Mr. Jacob Oppenheim, clockmaker, just a few minutes later. The proprietor of the shop, who was standing behind the counter, did not hide his surprise to see his former employer, as he asked, "Mr. Lyon, what brings you to Manchester?"

As Mr. Lyon still did not know how to begin, he began by saying, "You know Mr. Melamed, don't you, Jacob?"

"Yes, of course." Mr. Oppenheim bowed his head slightly in Mr. Melamed's direction. When neither of the two men spoke, Mr. Oppenheim said, "I hope nothing is wrong."

"I'm ruined, Jacob!" Mr. Lyon blurted out. "I've

lost everything in the Stock Exchange."

"What?"

"All I had left was one thousand guineas that I'd kept in my shop, and now that's gone, too. Someone stole it. I haven't got a ha'penny in the world, and Hannah wants to break off her engagement to Mr. Goldsmith, and..."

Mr. Lyon suddenly began to gasp for breath and his face turned quite pale. When he stumbled forward, Mr. Melamed caught him by the arm to prevent him from falling.

"Is there someplace where Mr. Lyon can sit down?" Mr. Melamed asked.

Mr. Oppenheim showed them to his back room, where there was a table and chair. He then brought Mr. Lyon a glass of wine. While Mr. Lyon was recovering, Mr. Oppenheim escorted Mr. Melamed back into the front room of the shop.

"I don't understand, Mr. Melamed. Has Mr. Lyon truly lost his entire fortune?"

"Yes, I'm afraid so."

"But why must the engagement be broken? Can't the community help?"

"Apparently, Miss Lyon does not wish to accept charity from the community."

"I see. But what does all this have to do with me?"

"Someone broke into Mr. Lyon's shop last week and stole his strongbox, which had within it one thousand guineas. We have reason to believe that the theft was committed by a man who was working in collaboration with the shop's messenger boy."

"Simon?"

"You were in London, Mr. Oppenheim, on the evening that the theft was committed."

Mr. Oppenheim stared at Mr. Melamed. "Does this mean that you suspect me of committing the theft?"

"I am making inquiries of anyone who might have been involved."

Mr. Oppenheim did not say anything for several minutes. Mr. Melamed tried to read what was going on behind the young man's eyes, but he wasn't sure if he was seeing anger, guilt, or some other emotion.

"If Mr. Lyon has lost his entire fortune, how will getting back the thousand guineas help him?"

It was a surprising question to ask, for in Mr. Melamed's opinion it had nothing to do with the real issue, which was returning the money to its rightful owner. However, he decided to answer it, if only to have a better idea of what was going on in the young man's mind.

"One thousand guineas is enough money for the Lyon family to live on for a year, without having to accept charity. If they economize, they could even pay for the wedding and a small portion of Miss Lyon's dowry. There's no guarantee that the

Goldsmith family would agree to go on with the wedding, even under these conditions. But even if the engagement is broken, at least the Lyon family wouldn't be paupers. That seems to be important, at least to Miss Lyon."

Mr. Oppenheim was once again silent. Mr. Melamed could see that there was some sort of struggle going on within the young man, but he wasn't exactly sure what it was.

"Simon is innocent," said Mr. Oppenheim, when he finally spoke. "You must promise me that you will not touch the child, or ask him anything more about this matter. Otherwise, I shall not help you."

"I give you my word."

There was yet another pause and then Mr. Oppenheim said, "I took the money."

Mr. Melamed did not speak, mainly because he did not know what to say. Perhaps he should have felt victorious at having discovered the identity of the thief. But if this was victory, it was a hollow one.

"I would prefer that you did not question me about my reasons, as they really don't matter," Mr. Oppenheim continued. "More to the point is how to return the money to Mr. Lyon. I have two hundred pounds currently in my possession. By this evening, I think I could get you three hundred **more. If you would be willing to loan me the** remaining five hundred pounds, I would endeavor to pay it back to you within three years."

"You have invested the money? Is that why you cannot pay back?"

"I am sorry, but this is the best that I can do and I cannot say more."

"Very well. I shall have the loan agreement ready by the time you bring the money to our inn."

"And, Mr. Melamed, I know that I am not in a position to make demands, but there is one thing more that I do request. Please do not tell Mr. Lyon anything about this until after you have left Manchester."

"Don't tell me what, Jacob?"

Both Mr. Oppenheim and Mr. Melamed turned to the door, where Mr. Lyon was standing.

"You're not well, Mr. Lyon. I think it best for Mr. Melamed to take you back to your inn."

"Jacob, what is it that you don't want me to know?"

Mr. Oppenheim looked from Mr. Lyon to Mr. Melamed. When he saw that Mr. Melamed was silent, he said, "I am sorry to have disappointed you, Mr. Lyon. You shall have your money this evening. Now, please, if you don't mind, I must ask you both to leave my shop."

✦ ✦ ✦

MR. LYON STARED INTO THE fire. His untouched supper lay on the table before him. "You think me a fool, don't you, to be so upset?" he asked Mr. Melamed, who had also barely tasted his food.

"At least you have back your money. You must be grateful for that."

"But he was like a son to me. I did everything I could for him. I wanted to see him succeed. If he had only asked me for the money, I would have given it to him. I would have taken out a loan, if I didn't have it, just as I would have done if it were my own son. If he needed money, why didn't he just ask?"

"I don't know. But the carriage will be here in a few minutes," said Mr. Melamed, as he glanced over at the inn's clock. "And you should eat something, Mr. Lyon. It's going to be a long trip back to London."

❖ ❖ ❖

THE DIFFICULT JOURNEY TOOK ITS toll on Mr. Lyon. However, it wasn't only the rigors of traveling that had depleted Mr. Lyon's strength. His heart had been broken by Mr. Oppenheim's betrayal, and he insisted that he should never be able to trust another man again.

His doctor, who assumed that Mr. Lyon's weak condition was only a physical ailment, ordered him to rest in bed for a week. "Then you will be back to your usual cheerful self," he said with a cheerful smile of his own.

"You could all do with a few weeks in Brighton," said the doctor, as he looked around at the pale faces of Mrs. Lyon and her two eldest daughters.

Of course, the doctor didn't know anything about the change in the Lyon family's fortunes, which made a pleasure trip to Brighton quite impossible. Neither did he know how much pain he had caused them by mentioning the name of that resort. For Brighton was very much at the root of their present distress, since Hannah still had not received a letter from Mr. David Goldsmith, Mr. Mayer Goldsmith, or anyone who answered to the name of Goldsmith.

"At least they could give us the courtesy of confirming that the wedding will not take place," said Mrs. Lyon, as she and her daughters sat in the sitting room after the doctor had left and they had finished their tea.

"It is quite clear that the wedding will not take place, Mama," said Hannah, "and so there is no reason for them to reply."

Despite what Hannah said, though, every day the family hoped that a letter would arrive. But every day those hopes were disappointed.

❖ ❖ ❖

MEANWHILE, A LETTER WAS DELIVERED to Mr. Melamed's home. When he opened it, he saw that it was from his business associate, Mr. Arthur Powell. Mr. Powell had apparently discovered some information that he thought might be of use to Mr. Melamed.

Since the thief had been found and the money had been returned, his first thought was to tell Mr. Powell that his information was no longer needed. But no sooner did he pick up his pen than he set it down. It was true that the thief had been found and the money had been returned. Mr. Oppenheim had kept his word and brought five hundred pounds to the inn. The young man had signed the loan agreement for the remaining five hundred pounds, and the agreement had been witnessed by the innkeeper and a businessman staying at the inn, a person who was known to the innkeeper and so could be relied upon to be a kosher witness. So when everything was in order, why did Mr. Melamed still feel so unsettled, he wondered? Why was there still a part of him that believed that the mystery still hadn't been solved?

The question from the Talmud once again entered his mind: What is the law if a mouse enters a house with a piece of bread in its mouth and a mouse leaves with a piece of bread in its mouth? Do we say that the mouse that entered is the one that left, or is it a different mouse?

Was it really possible, he wondered, that Mr. Oppenheim, who had been treated by his employer as a son, would repay Mr. Lyon with an act of theft? Or, Mr. Melamed wondered, had he inadvertently trapped the wrong mouse?

Chapter Fifteen

"It's more than i thought I'd discover," said Mr. Powell, looking more than a little pleased about having stumbled upon an interesting piece of information. "Fortunately, the horse dealer at Tattersall's was in a talkative mood."

"If I owe you anything for the ale, let me know," said Mr. Melamed.

Mr. Powell laughed. "I won't charge you for the drinks, but I might make you pay for the doctor's visit afterward. That ale quite ruined my digestive system, and I was supposed to dine in Brighton that evening with the Duke of York."

"I hope the Duke excused you for your absence.

I'd hate to see you lose not only your dinner, but also your head because of this."

"Believe it or not, the Duke does get into a huff when someone he has invited to one of his dinner parties doesn't turn up. However, I'm just barely important enough for him to snub, and so I think he will find it more convenient to forget all about it. But let's get back to this business of yours, shall we?"

"I have no objection."

"Mr. Grenville did, indeed, purchase that pair of greys I told you about. He paid three hundred pounds for them. He was robbed, of course, because they weren't worth more than two hundred and fifty. However, what was interesting about the purchase, in my opinion, was that the horses weren't for him."

"Who were they for?"

"That's not something that is important for you to know. What is important, though, is that the horses were payment for a gambling debt that Mr. Grenville owed. It seems that he had made a bet with a gentleman about something or another, and whoever lost the bet had to pay with a pair of greys. As I am sure you are aware, a gentleman can leave a tradesman's bill unpaid for half a dozen years. However, when it comes to a bet made with another gentleman, the debt must be paid immediately."

"Did Mr. Grenville have any other gambling

debts that he needed to pay?"

"If my source at Tattersall's is as knowledgeable as he pretends to be, Percy Grenville is on the verge of being blackballed by his fashionable friends for that very reason. He owes money to everyone."

"What about his father, Lord Grenville? Wouldn't he pay off the debts, to preserve the honor of the family name?"

"He used to, but he's not willing to do it anymore. At least that's what our horse dealer friend says."

"So would it be fair to say that Mr. Grenville is a desperate man?"

"One could say that. But be careful, Melamed. Be very careful. Lord Grenville is a good friend to have. It would be a pity to turn him into an enemy."

"And if Mr. Grenville should steal again? Should we just let him do it?"

"I'm not saying that. What I am saying, though, is that if you do plan to go to Lord Grenville and accuse his son of stealing, your proof for such an astonishing accusation must be very, very good."

◆ ◆ ◆

"THAT'S THE PROBLEM, ISN'T IT? You haven't got any proof."

Mr. Melamed took a sip from his cup of coffee.

He was grateful to be able to talk things over with Asher Baer, but once again they didn't seem to be getting anywhere.

"Yes, that is the problem," Mr. Melamed replied. "The only evidence I have is the button. And as you've already mentioned, the button could have fallen off when Grenville's servants brought the clock into Mr. Lyon's back room."

"Still, it is suspicious. The money that Lord Grenville paid for the clocks was exactly three hundred pounds, which was exactly the amount of money that the young Grenville needed for his horses."

"Suspicions aren't proof."

Mrs. Baer came down the stairs and began to tidy up the room. It was evening, and almost time for the coffee house to close its doors. When she spotted Mr. Melamed talking with her husband, she came over to the table.

"Mr. Melamed, I didn't know you were here."

"Good evening, Mrs. Baer. I hope you are well."

"I am as well as I can be with two children coughing, another two sniffling, and the youngest one running a fever. But I hope that won't stop you from coming to us for Shabbos, as usual."

"G-d willing, I'll be there."

"Good. I'll get back to clearing away these dishes, if you'll excuse me."

When Mrs. Baer had moved to another part

of the room, Mr. Melamed asked, "Does she know about Jacob Oppenheim?"

"No. It would break her heart if she found out that he was a thief. And I'm not going to break her heart, if it was really Lord Button who committed the crime."

"I have no proof, Asher."

"Maybe you do, Mr. Melamed, but you're just not seeing it."

✦ ✦ ✦

ALTHOUGH THE DOCTOR HAD TOLD Mr. Lyon to rest for a week, Mr. Lyon did not like to be away from his business for so long. And so after only a few days he paid a visit to his shop. He was pleased to see that Mr. Warburg had kept the shop clean and orderly. He was further pleased to see that a wealthy banker had put in an order for a longcase clock for his library and another one for his dining room. There were also a few orders for mantle clocks, and everything had been entered neatly into the account book by Mr. Warburg.

After he finished inspecting the shop, Mr. Lyon paid a visit to the warehouse. There, as well, everything seemed to be running smoothly.

"We've fixed the problem with Lord Grenville's clock," Mr. Abramson informed him. "It can be sent to the townhouse whenever you say."

"I am under the impression that the townhouse has been closed up, now that the London season has ended."

"So what does he expect us to do with the clock? Keep it here until next spring?"

"I really don't know, Mr. Abramson. But that is a very good question. I shall let you know when I have an answer."

"I can take a message to the house right now, sir," said Simon, who had been standing nearby.

Mr. Lyon looked at the boy, and became filled with remorse for having suspected the child's innocence for even a moment. He had brought with him a small token of friendship, which he handed to the child as he said, "It can wait until tomorrow. Here's a piece of seedcake to have with your tea."

After he gave the boy the piece of cake, he turned to Mr. Abramson. "I am feeling a little tired, and so I shall return home now."

"Shall I find you a carriage?"

"No, thank you. I shall walk. But if you need me for anything, send Simon."

"Yes, Mr. Lyon."

Although Mr. Lyon was feeling quite exhausted and should have hired a carriage to take him back to Devonshire Square, he didn't want to spend money on such an extravagance. He therefore set out on foot, deciding that he would walk slowly **to conserve his strength. Because he had arrived** at the shop when it was already late afternoon, the light was starting to fade by the time he reached the point where Threadneedle Street intersected with Bishopsgate. His strength was fading, as well, but he was not tempted to turn inside the Bull Inn, or the Green Dragon, or the Four Swans Inn to rest. All he wanted to do was to reach his own home, where his own bed was waiting for him.

It was already quite dark when he reached Houndsditch. Although he knew that it was safer to stay on the main road, he was very tired, and so he decided to take the shortcut through Fall Alley, which connected Houndsditch with Devonshire Square. But his shortcut turned out to be the long way to his home, because fall he did in that dark alley, although he did not know how. All he could say, afterward, was that all of a sudden two — or perhaps it was three — men appeared from out of the shadows and pounced upon him, throwing him so quickly to the ground that he did not have a chance to see the men's faces. All he felt were their blows, which rained down upon him with such force that he wasn't sure if he would survive them.

"Stop looking for the man who stole your thousand guineas," one of the men snarled in his ear. "Promise or I'll slit your throat."

Mr. Lyon wanted to promise, but it was difficult for him to speak because his assailant had grasped **him by the very throat that he threatened to slit.**

As Mr. Lyon tried to explain that he could barely breathe, let alone talk, his eye caught sight of the knife being wielded in his assailant's free hand. Sure that his life was over, Mr. Lyon tried to scream, "*Shema Yisrael!*" But here too he was thwarted, for suddenly, from out of the darkness, he heard a young voice cry out, "Charge!"

Within an instant, the alley was filled with the sounds of a ferocious battle. Or so it seemed to Mr. Lyon's ears, for he was too weak to raise his battered limbs from the ground and actually see what was transpiring.

When the battle seemed to have come to an end — for Mr. Lyon could hear the sound of heavy footsteps quickly retreating down the alley — Mr. Lyon heard a familiar voice whisper in his ear, "Are you all right, Mr. Lyon?"

"Simon?" he managed to gasp.

"I followed you home, sir. I hope you don't mind that I left the shop early. But I was afraid that you were going to topple over somewhere on Bishopsgate. You looked real pale."

"Help him up, men," a voice said, and Mr. Lyon suddenly felt himself being raised to his feet.

"I don't think I can walk," Mr. Lyon said, after he tried to take a step.

"You will take him home, General Well'ngone, won't you?" asked Simon.

"My men usually don't provide that sort of

service," Well'ngone replied. "But I suppose no harm will come out of our doing your employer a favor."

"I shall pay you for your assistance," said Mr. Lyon.

"Squire, we know all about your situation. Your pockets are even emptier than ours, so don't start blathering about payment. But you should do something nice for young Simon, when you're back on your feet again. He's the one who alerted us to your wandering around alone in the East End after dark. And really, Squire, a man of your age should know better than to do a foolish thing like that."

Well'ngone ordered his men to march, and after several minutes they reached the home of Mr. Lyon. When Perl opened the door she gasped, because Mr. Lyon's clothes were all torn and bloody. Fortunately, she kept her wits about her and she did not immediately inform Mrs. Lyon, who would surely have collapsed into a fit of hysterics to see Mr. Lyon in such a sorry state. Instead, she ran to fetch her father, the family's manservant, Meshullam Mendel, and it was he, assisted by Simon, who helped Mr. Lyon up the stairs and to his room.

By the time the family had been informed of what had happened, and rushed to the front door to thank the boys who had saved Mr. Lyon from danger, the front step was empty. Well'ngone and his men had disappeared into the night.

◆ ◆ ◆

MR. MELAMED WAS READING IN his library when he heard the front bell ring. He could also hear the sound of his butler's footsteps as the man walked down the hallway to answer the door, for his house was that quiet. Then, surprisingly, for the hour was already late, no sooner had the butler begun his journey back down the hallway and to the library than the front bell rang again.

When his butler came into the library, Mr. Melamed saw that the man had in his hand a small silver tray, upon which two letters were sitting.

"Two letters? At this hour?" he commented.

"Yes, sir. They both came by messenger."

His butler placed the letters on the desk and departed. While the man's echoing footsteps faded into silence, Mr. Melamed studied the two letters. One was from Mr. Lyon. The other one had been sent from the Continent.

He decided to read Mr. Lyon's letter first, and he was quite surprised by its contents. It seemed impossible even to him that Mr. Oppenheim would hire a pair of cutthroats and threaten to take Mr. Lyon's life. It also seemed improbable that Percy Grenville would take such a drastic step. Yet someone connected to the theft had to have done it, since the threat was quite specific.

As he had no answer to the questions raised by Mr. Lyon's letter, he turned his attention to the second letter, which was from his son-in-law's Rebbe. If his letter to the holy man had been brief, the Rebbe's reply was even briefer. And to Mr. Melamed's great disappointment, the reply was so cryptic that it didn't seem to solve a thing, for all that the Rebbe had written were these words:

Watch the clock.

Chapter Sixteen

THE NEXT MORNING MR. MELAMED received a second letter from Mr. Lyon, which begged him to pay a visit to Devonshire Square at his earliest convenience, as there was something very urgent that they needed to discuss. Mr. Melamed therefore arrived at the Lyons' home after breakfast.

"Mr. Melamed, would you please tell my husband that he must rest," said Mrs. Lyon, as she escorted Mr. Melamed to the library. "I begged him to stay in bed this morning, but he will not listen to me."

"I will try to convince him."

Mrs. Lyon showed their guest into the library and then shut the door so that the two men could speak in private. Mr. Melamed was very shocked to see Mr. Lyon, for the clockmaker's face was quite bruised and Mr. Melamed assumed that much of the rest of the unfortunate man's body was colored a similar shade of purple. However, he did note that Mr. Lyon seemed to be animated with a new energy, and he soon discovered the reason for the change in the man's spirits.

"This proves it, Mr. Melamed. I don't care what you, my wife, or even what Mr. Oppenheim says. Jacob Oppenheim did not take the money."

"I'm inclined to agree with you. But why did Mr. Oppenheim say he did it, if it wasn't true?"

"I don't know, and we can find that out later. But we must find the real thief."

"Have you any idea who attacked you last night?"

"No. Neither does Simon or Well'ngone."

"You've spoken to Well'ngone?"

"I spoke to Simon. He says that all they know is that the men were foreigners."

"Foreigners?"

"They weren't from the Jewish part of the East End."

"Ah. That doesn't give us much to go on, then, since most people in London would fit that description."

"If we could only link my attackers to Percy Grenville," said Mr. Lyon, a bit wistfully.

"I'll go to Fall Alley and have a look around. Perhaps they left something behind."

"Simon and Well'ngone have already done that. They didn't find a thing."

"Still, it won't hurt anything for me to also take a look."

Mr. Melamed had a meeting that he had to attend at the Great Synagogue, but he thought he might have a quarter of an hour to conduct his search. He therefore glanced over at the longcase clock that stood in Mr. Lyon's study to check the time. To his surprise, the clock told him that he had more than three-quarters of an hour to devote to searching Fall Alley.

"Is your clock accurate, Mr. Lyon?"

"It should be."

Mr. Melamed took out his pocket watch and checked it against the time of the clock. "I suppose my watch must be running fast."

"No, listen. The tall clock has stopped ticking. That's very strange. I wound it up yesterday, myself, before I left for the shop."

Mr. Melamed suddenly recalled the words of the Rebbe's letter: *Watch the clock*. He sat for a few moments and watched the longcase clock, but without having any idea of what he was supposed to be seeing.

"Is it normal for a clock to suddenly stop ticking, Mr. Lyon?"

"Not if it's properly made and if the weights are kept wound up."

"The weights are located inside the case, are they not?"

"Yes, I'll show you."

Mr. Lyon walked over to the clock. Fortunately, he did not have to walk far, as each step he took was very painful.

"That's why the case has to be so tall, to accommodate the pendulum and the weights," Mr. Lyon explained as he opened the case's door. "The longer the pendulum is, the more accurate the... Joshua! What are you doing hiding inside this clock? You get out of there at once!"

Joshua scampered out from his hiding place and ran to hide behind Mr. Melamed's chair.

"But, Papa, what's a fellow supposed to do? Everyone's walking around the house with their faces down to the floor and no one will tell me why. I'm a member of this family. I want to know what's happened, too."

"That's no excuse, young man. You must get out of this bad habit of yours of listening in on other people's private conversations. Isn't that right, Mr. Melamed?"

"I agree with you, Mr. Lyon, entirely. But you do realize, don't you, that Joshua has just solved our mystery for us?"

❖ ❖ ❖

MR. MELAMED SENT WORD TO the Great Synagogue
that he would not be able to attend the meeting.
Instead, he set out for Cornhill, accompanied by
Mr. Lyon and Joshua. Perl had placed extra pillows
in the carriage for Mr. Lyon to sit on, and so the
ride was not overly taxing for him. After greeting
Mr. Warburg, they went into the back room,
where Mr. Melamed took charge and began to test
his theory, which was that a child had been hidden
inside the longcase clock that Mr. Percy Grenville's
servants had brought into the back room of Mr.
Lyon's shop.

"Joshua, you get inside the clock," he said, as he
opened the case of the clock.

"Yes, Mr. Melamed. This one is much roomier
than the clock we have at home. A fellow could sit
in here for hours when the weights are up."

"That's what I'm thinking, as well," said Mr.
Melamed, as he closed the case's door. "Now, you,
Mr. Lyon, will sit at your desk."

"Very well," Mr. Lyon replied, as he carefully
lowered his body onto the wooden chair.

"I'd like you to bend over and remove the
floorboard and the strongbox."

"I'm sorry, but I don't think I can bend down."

"We'll change places then."

Mr. Lyon got up and Mr. Melamed sat down on

the chair. "Joshua, if you can see anything through the keyhole, tell me what you see."

"Yes, Mr. Melamed."

Mr. Melamed bent down and lifted up the floorboard.

"It looks like you've got some sort of board in your hand," said Joshua.

Mr. Melamed put the plank of wood on the floor. When he realized that the hiding place was empty, he turned to the desk and opened a drawer and took out the key.

"You've opened the drawer and taken out a key," a muffled little voice called out.

"Very good, Joshua. Keep watching."

Mr. Melamed then bent down, as though he was putting the key in the hole. However, instead of lifting up the key again, he took out his handkerchief and raised that up instead.

"You're waving your handkerchief."

"Excellent," said Mr. Melamed, as he walked over to the longcase clock and opened the door. "Thank you, Joshua, you've been very helpful."

Mr. Melamed then turned to Mr. Lyon and said, "Whoever was hiding inside that clock saw almost everything you did while you were sitting at this desk. Although he couldn't have known exactly where the loose floorboard was located, he knew that it was somewhere nearby."

"But what about the key? I didn't remove the key."

"That was probably a bit of luck that the child found it in the desk. But even if the child hadn't found the key, once he was already inside the shop he could have slipped the money through the bars of the window. Then he could have either found a way to unlock the door from the inside or waited in his hiding place until morning, when he could have escaped, unnoticed, once you opened the back door."

"But who was this child?"

"It wasn't a child," said Joshua, who had been listening to the grown-ups' conversation very carefully.

"Why do you say that?" asked Mr. Melamed.

"Look over here, at the keyhole." Joshua led Mr. Melamed over to the clock and reopened the door of the case. "There's some white hairs stuck to it. What fellow like me has white hair?"

❖ ❖ ❖

AFTER ASCERTAINING FROM MR. LYON that Lord Grenville had a longcase clock in his Brighton townhouse, for the gentleman insisted upon having all the comforts of home in all of his many homes, Mr. Melamed sent Mr. Lyon and Joshua back to Devonshire Square in his carriage. He then obtained a place on a mail coach to Brighton, with **the intention of paying a visit to Lord Grenville at** the nobleman's summer residence. Mr. Melamed was very aware that the only actual evidence he had to link Percy Grenville with the theft was the button sitting in his waistcoat pocket, and that even the button was only circumstantial evidence. The rest of his theory was pure conjecture. However, he reassured himself that since his purpose was to restore Mr. Lyon's money to its rightful owner, surely the One Who guides our steps would lead him along the correct path.

He did hesitate for a moment before placing his hand upon the perfectly polished door knocker that ornamented the impressive front door of Lord Grenville's townhouse, which was located in the most fashionable part of Brighton. He also was aware, after the impeccably correct footman came to the door and took his visiting card, that a part of him secretly wished that the nobleman had been called away from Brighton for some reason, so that he could postpone the meeting to another time. However, when the footman returned to the front door and informed Mr. Melamed that Lord Grenville was at home, he knew he had no choice except to follow the footman into the richly furnished drawing room. There his name was announced and the footman discreetly disappeared.

"I believe I met you last year, Mr. Melamed, when the Royal Dukes attended a service at your

Great Synagogue," said Lord Grenville, as he motioned to Mr. Melamed to take a seat.

"I am flattered that you remember, Lord Grenville."

"What can I do for you? I assume that is why you are here, because you need my assistance."

"Someone has broken into the shop of Mr. Samuel Lyon and stolen his strongbox," replied Mr. Melamed, deciding to get straight to the business at hand, before Lord Grenville lost interest and he lost resolve. "It had in it one thousand guineas."

"Samuel Lyon? The clockmaker on Cornhill Street?"

"Yes, that's the one."

"I'm sorry to hear it, but I can't see how this has anything to do with me. I suggest you notify the magistrate's office. If they're slow about getting the Bow Street Runners on the case, you can mention my name, if that will help."

"Thank you, but I would prefer not to go to the authorities, Lord Grenville."

"Why not?"

"Because I have reason to believe that the person who stole the money was your son."

Mr. Melamed watched as the benevolent expression that had been on Lord Grenville's face disappeared. At first, the nobleman just stared at Mr. Melamed with disbelief. Then the man's face began to turn a distinct shade of red, as he struggled not to leap from his chair — Mr. Melamed suddenly recalled that Lord Grenville had been a military man in his younger days and was still considered to be an excellent horseman — and throttle Mr. Melamed for his impertinence.

Mr. Melamed knew that the next few minutes were crucial. If he did not succeed in convincing Lord Grenville to at least entertain the possibility that his seemingly audacious accusation was true, not only would Mr. Lyon not get back his money, but the Jewish community would lose one of its most powerful allies. He also knew that he had only one weapon in his arsenal to fight Lord Grenville's rage: silence. For surely if Mr. Melamed's suspicions were correct, he reasoned, Lord Grenville must also have had some suspicions about his son. How, for example, did the young man obtain the money to buy horses and continue with his other profligate activities, if Lord Grenville had cut off his son's allowance?

Mr. Melamed therefore did not say a word, even though he was sorely tempted to blurt out some hasty apology to make amends. He also forced himself to not even look at Lord Grenville and meet the challenge of those glaring eyes. If he showed fear, uncertainty, or anger of his own, he was lost. And so instead, Mr. Melamed kept his eyes firmly affixed upon the longcase clock that was in the drawing room, and whose impassive face loomed just above Lord Grenville's right shoulder. *Watch the clock*, the Rebbe had told him. That advice had helped him to solve the mystery of how one of the "mice" — the child — had gotten into the shop. Now he would use that advice to try and catch the instigator of the theft, Lord Grenville's son.

Mr. Melamed compelled himself to regulate his breathing according to the ticking of the clock, and this action calmed both his worried thoughts and the frantic beating of his heart. In the silence, where only the ticking of the clock was heard, he noted that Lord Grenville's breathing was also slowly beginning to calm down. Mr. Melamed correctly guessed that the nobleman's mottled face was beginning to be drained of its bright red color.

After a very long silence, Lord Grenville asked, quietly and reasonably, "What is your proof, Mr. Melamed?"

"The theft occurred on the same day that you sent your longcase clock to Mr. Lyon's shop for repair."

"I sent...? Why would I send the clock for repair? There was nothing wrong with it when I left for Brighton."

Mr. Melamed did not smile, but inwardly he rejoiced. All he had to do was unravel Percy Grenville's plot stitch by stitch, and then, if Lord Grenville was an honorable man, the nobleman **would do the rest. "Then you didn't ask your son to** take the clock to Mr. Lyon's shop, or to pay the bill, which I believe was for three hundred guineas?"

"Of course not. I asked my secretary to send a message to Mr. Lyon and tell him to come to the townhouse to pick up the money. And I can assure you that my secretary would not mistake my son for a messenger."

Blotches of red had returned to Lord Grenville's face. However, Mr. Melamed forced himself to remain calm and not let himself become affected by the nobleman's anger.

"It is possible that Mr. Lyon might have mistaken the identity of the young man who came to his shop," he said evenly. "Perhaps the young man was really one of your servants, and he was impersonating Mr. Grenville. At any rate, the two servants who came with this young man and brought the clock into Mr. Lyon's back room belonged to your household. For one of the servants left behind this."

Mr. Melamed removed the button from his waistcoat pocket and handed it to Lord Grenville. Then he held his breath. It was such flimsy evidence, and yet it was proof that someone associated with Lord Grenville had been to the shop.

Lord Grenville took the button and examined it for several minutes, as though the insignia impressed upon the metal was a piece of hieroglyphics and not a design that he was quite familiar with. When he finally did speak, his voice was almost a whisper.

"The button belongs to my household. And I will admit that it is strange that someone from my household brought the clock to Mr. Lyon's shop. But this button doesn't prove that my son, or one of my servants, stole money from Mr. Lyon."

"I am aware of that, Lord Grenville. But may I take the liberty of asking you a few questions?"

Lord Grenville was not happy to give his permission, but he signaled with a nod of his head that Mr. Melamed could continue.

"Does your son have, by any chance, a young child in his service who comes from a foreign country?"

The angry glare returned to Lord Grenville's eyes. However, this time it was not directed at Mr. Melamed.

"He does, to my displeasure. He bought a child from the French West Indies, Antoine, whom he's dressed up as his page. I don't approve at all of the slave trade, or of treating these children from the West Indies like they're pet monkeys."

"Are your son and the page here at the moment?"

"I assume so. It's only two o'clock in the afternoon. My son is probably still having his breakfast."

"Then with your permission, this is what I would like to do to prove the accuracy of my words."

Mr. Melamed explained his stratagem to Lord Grenville, who approved the plan. Mr. Percy Grenville's page was summoned and instructed to hide inside the longcase clock that was in Lord Grenville's drawing room.

"It's very crowded, sir," said the child, as he adjusted his white wig. "I can barely fit inside."

"Is it more crowded than the clock in London?" asked Lord Grenville, obviously hoping that the child would not know what he was talking about.

"Much more," replied the child.

Lord Grenville looked over at Mr. Melamed, who was being very meticulous about not showing any signs of joy over this new confirmation of the correctness of his suspicions.

After the door to the clock was closed, Lord Grenville summoned the footman and asked that Mr. Percy Grenville be informed that he was wanted in the drawing room. When the young man arrived, still dressed in his silk dressing gown, Lord Grenville explained the charges being brought against him, but without explaining Mr. Melamed's theory as to how the crime had been committed. The young man yawned.

"Really, Father, don't tell me that you actually believe this man's story. It's a case of blackmail, pure and simple."

"So you didn't break into the shop?" asked Lord Grenville.

"I'm shocked to even be asked such a question."

"And your page?"

"Antoine?"

"*Allez! Allez!*" Mr. Melamed suddenly called out.

The door to the case popped open and Antoine stepped outside.

"*Surprise!*"

Mr. Percy Grenville stared first at Antoine, and then at Mr. Melamed. Then he sprang from his chair, and as he lunged at Mr. Melamed, he snarled, "Why, you ..."

He did not finish his sentence, for Lord Grenville grabbed him from behind and dragged the young man out of the drawing room by the collar of his expensive silk dressing gown.

❖ ❖ ❖

WHILE MR. MELAMED WAITED IN Lord Grenville's drawing room, Mr. and Mrs. Lyon were receiving surprise visitors of their own in their drawing room in Devonshire Square.

"Would you care for some cake, Mr. Goldsmith?" asked Mrs. Lyon, trying very hard to keep both her voice and hand from shaking.

"Thank you, Mrs. Lyon."

When the cups of coffee and pieces of cake

had been passed around to Mr. Mayer Goldsmith and Mr. David Goldsmith — Mrs. Goldsmith had remained in Brighton — there was an uncomfortable silence.

"There's no need to explain," said Mr. Lyon, finally breaking that silence. "We understand your decision entirely."

"Excuse me for asking, Mr. Lyon," said Mr. David Goldsmith, "but if you haven't heard our decision, how can you understand it?"

❖ ❖ ❖

MEANWHILE, THE LYON CHILDREN WERE upstairs, where they were waiting very decorously to hear the outcome of the very interesting conversation taking place in the drawing room. Hannah sat by the window, looking listlessly into the air. Rebecca was staring at the pages of one of her favorite books, and imaging every possible disaster. The two younger Miss Lyons, Esther and Sarah, were fighting over some pieces of clothing for their dolls. And as for Joshua, there was no danger of the little boy sneaking into the drawing room and listening unawares, because Rebecca had tied one end of a piece of rope to his ankle and the other end around the leg of a cupboard, and so he couldn't go far.

When they heard the front door slam shut and the sound of their parents' footsteps on the stairs, the children sprang to their feet. But when Rebecca saw the serious look on her father's face, she thought she was going to faint and collapse onto the floor. Midday or not, she was sure that she had never been so frightened in her life, as she was certain that her deepest fears had come true: Mr. David Goldsmith had broken off his engagement to Hannah and given his hand to another.

Before she fainted, though, Rebecca stole a look over at Hannah. Her sister was trying very hard to be brave, but everyone could see that Hannah's chin was trembling and that little tears had formed at the corners of her eyes. Rebecca therefore realized that she really couldn't faint, at least not at that moment. It was for Hannah to faint, if anyone was to do it. Her role was to tend to Hannah, should her assistance be required. And Rebecca was certain that her assistance would be required when she returned her gaze to Mr. Lyon, who was looking more solemn than she had ever seen him look in her entire life.

Mr. Lyon was, in turn, looking at the little group, whose faces were all turned to him. Then he said, softly, "I'm sorry, Hannah. I tried to convince the Goldsmiths. Truly I did. But I couldn't do it. Mr. David Goldsmith absolutely refuses to...break off the engagement."

Mr. Lyon started to laugh, and Mrs. Lyon started to cry. Hannah couldn't say or do anything at first, but then she flew into her father's arms, and Mr. Lyon gave her a big hug. Then Hannah hugged Mrs. Lyon, and soon everyone was hugging everyone else, and after the family finished with hugging and crying they all went downstairs to have their tea.

"Hey!" shouted Joshua, who was still tied to the cupboard. "What about me?"

Chapter Seventeen

Mr. melamed waited in lord Grenville's drawing room until the footman returned and said, "Lord Grenville apologizes for the delay. He requests your presence in the library."

Mr. Melamed followed the footman down the long hallway, which was adorned with a series of landscape murals painted on the walls. The hallway ended with a door that led to Lord Grenville's library. This library was no *trompe l'oeil*, where titles of books had been painted on pieces of leather that covered nothing more than an empty shell. The thousands of books were real, and this was just Lord Grenville's summer home. Mr.

Melamed was impressed, but he knew that this was not the time to make a study of the nobleman's book collection.

"Have a seat, Mr. Melamed," said Lord Grenville, who was seated at his desk and writing something.

"Thank you."

"I am sending Percy to Spain. Perhaps Wellington will have more success with turning him into a worthwhile member of the human race than I've had."

Mr. Melamed did not say anything. However, he understood that Mr. Percy Grenville's upcoming military service was meant to be a punishment, in lieu of serving a sentence in Newgate Prison.

"And this is for Mr. Lyon," said Lord Grenville, as he handed the piece of paper to Mr. Melamed. "He may take it to my bank in London, and they will redeem it for cash."

"There has been a mistake," replied Mr. Melamed, as he looked down at the sum written in the letter. "Only one thousand guineas were taken from Mr. Lyon's shop. This is for much more."

"I know. But I am assuming that the theft caused Mr. Lyon some distress. Otherwise, you wouldn't have risked coming to me. And then there is that other business. My son didn't know you hadn't told me about the two men he sent to threaten Mr. Lyon, so he confessed to that, as well. So consider the additional twenty thousand pounds to be my way of making amends to Mr. Lyon and his family for my son's rather despicable behavior."

✦ ✦ ✦

"TWENTY THOUSAND POUNDS?" ASKED MRS. Lyon, at first not comprehending the news she had just heard. "Twenty thousand pounds!"

"We're rich again!" exclaimed Rebecca, who was just as surprised and delighted as her mother. "Mr. Melamed, you were right! Everything can change in a blink of an eye! We must never give up hope! Never!"

While Rebecca Lyon shouted out her happiness in this very unladylike manner, her sister Hannah behaved exactly as a Daughter of Israel should. She was the very picture of a demure young lady as she thanked Mr. Melamed, in a low voice, for all his assistance and wished him continued success in his work on behalf of the community.

Mr. Lyon, meanwhile, seemed to not hear the happy tumult taking place all around him in his drawing room. He kept staring at the letter from Lord Grenville, not quite believing that it was real. However, when he did rouse himself from his thoughts, his face looked quite serious.

"Mr. Melamed, if the thief really was Percy Grenville, what about..."

"I've ordered a coach for tomorrow."

❖ ❖ ❖

THE COACH AND FOUR SPED through glen and dale, and eighteen hours later Mr. Lyon and Mr. Melamed were back in Manchester. This time it was Mr. Lyon who did not wish to linger at the inn where they stopped to refresh themselves after the long journey.

"We must get to the bottom of this at once," said Mr. Lyon, as he hurried toward the little clock shop.

Once again, Mr. Oppenheim was taken by surprise. But before he could say a word, Mr. Lyon said, "Sir, you have lied to me. You did not steal the money. The real thief has been found and I have regained my entire fortune. What do you have to say for yourself, sir?"

Mr. Oppenheim turned to Mr. Melamed. Although he did not speak, his eyes showed that he was requesting confirmation for Mr. Lyon's very strange outburst.

"What Mr. Lyon has said is true. Here are your five hundred guineas."

Mr. Melamed placed a heavy pouch on the counter, which was filled with coins. He then gave Mr. Oppenheim the loan agreement between them, which had been marked with the word "Void."

"Well, Mr. Oppenheim, we are waiting for an explanation," said Mr. Lyon, trying his best to look stern.

"I had to help you, Mr. Lyon," said Mr. Oppenheim, who was looking quite embarrassed to have been caught committing such a noble act. "When I saw how distressed you were, and when you told me that your daughter's engagement might be broken, because Miss Lyon did not wish to be dependent upon charity, I had to do something to help you. And so I said I was the thief."

"But where did you get the money from?" asked Mr. Lyon.

"I had two hundred pounds in the bank, which was money that I had been able to save. I borrowed three hundred pounds from a business acquaintance of mine here in Manchester. And then I borrowed the other five hundred pounds from Mr. Melamed, as you know."

"But why, Jacob? Why did you allow yourself to go into so much debt on my behalf?"

"But Mr. Lyon, if I had been the one who was in trouble, wouldn't you have done the same thing for me?"

Mr. Lyon took out his handkerchief and mopped his brow, too overwhelmed to speak.

"There's one thing I don't understand, Mr. Oppenheim," said Mr. Melamed. "Why could you not tell Mr. Lyon your business in London?"

"It's embarrassing for me to speak about it now, but I once had the hope that if I owned my own shop and proved that I could be successful, then

Mr. Lyon would grant me the privilege of marrying his eldest daughter. That is why I came to London. Because my business has been blessed with some success, and so I hoped... But when I heard from Mrs. Baer that the young lady was already engaged to another man, I... All I wanted to do was return to Manchester as quickly as I could."

◆ ◆ ◆

THAT EVENING MR. OPPENHEIM JOINED Mr. Lyon and Mr. Melamed for supper at the inn. Although much of the congenial conversation revolved around the business of making and selling mechanical clocks, every once in a while Mr. Lyon grew pensive and asked, "Are you sure you can forgive me, Jacob? It's a terrible thing to suspect any innocent man of a crime. How much more so to suspect a man whom you know in your heart to be honest!"

Mr. Oppenheim assured Mr. Lyon that he forgave him. However, Mr. Lyon was still not entirely reassured, and so when the carriage pulled into the inn's courtyard, he said, "You will come to the wedding, Jacob, won't you? That's the only way I will know that you have truly forgiven me, for everything."

"I shall try, Mr. Lyon," Mr. Oppenheim replied. "G-d willing, I will be there."

✦ ✦ ✦

WHILE MRS. LYON WAS BUSY with the final preparations for the wedding, Mr. Lyon had one more important call to make. And once again, he called upon Mr. Melamed to assist him. "You know where this Earl of Gravel Lane lives, and so I would be very much obliged if you would show me the way."

Mr. Melamed was not entirely surprised that Mr. Lyon wished to thank the Earl and Well'ngone for coming to his assistance in Fall Alley. And because he had a little business of his own to do in Gravel Lane, he readily agreed to join Mr. Lyon and make the visit together.

"By the way, I spoke to Simon about the account book," Mr. Lyon said to Mr. Melamed, as they walked across Petticoat Square. "He told me he was trying to practice his letters. I've bought him a reading primer for him to use instead."

"I'm glad that detail has been satisfactorily explained."

"I feel terrible for having suspected the child."

"I do, too."

"Do you think the synagogue could find a place for Simon in the Talmud Torah? He does seem rather keen to learn, and I would be happy to pay for part of his tuition."

"I'll look into it this afternoon."

By then Mr. Melamed and Mr. Lyon had reached Gravel Lane, where they were already well-known figures. They therefore had no trouble receiving permission to call upon the Earl. Well'ngone escorted the two men into the Earl's private room, where the Earl was already waiting to receive them.

"I hear you have caught your thief, Mr. Melamed," said the Earl. "Congratulations."

"Thank you. And I believe this guinea belongs to one of your group," Mr. Melamed replied, as he handed the guinea to Well'ngone. "It was General Well'ngone who witnessed the theft, wasn't it? I'm assuming he was on his way home, perhaps after an evening of picking people's pockets in Covent Garden? Simon only came to you the following morning, when he realized that the money had been stolen and he might be suspected of being the thief."

"Thieves don't involve themselves in the work of other thieves," said the Earl, "if you're wondering why General Well'ngone didn't stop the man and the boy from stealing the money. It was only afterward, when I realized that the theft involved Simon's employer, that I decided to assist you with your investigation."

The Earl took out his tin snuffbox from his pocket and made a show of taking a pinch of snuff. "You're a clever man, Mr. Melamed. If you ever need work, come to me and I'll see what I can do for you."

Mr. Lyon looked from Mr. Melamed to the Earl, not comprehending what the two were talking about. "If Mr. Melamed needs work? Mr. Melamed doesn't need work. It's you boys that need work. You need decent jobs, where you can earn a decent living and live in a decent home. That's why I've come here. I've decided to open up a new line of business and make pocket watches. You boys all have nimble fingers. You'll be excellent at it."

"One minute, Squire," said Well'ngone. "You want us to put something into people's pockets?"

"Yes. Pocket watches."

"The man's gone wobbly in the head," said Well'ngone, as he turned to the others and shook his head, as if commiserating with Mr. Lyon's unhappy state. The boys also shook their heads and wrung their hands and sighed, on cue.

"You mark my words, young man," said Mr. Lyon. "I'm not giving up on you. I'm not giving up on any of you. You have good hearts, all of you. I'm going to turn you into honest men if it takes me the rest of my life. And I expect all of you to be at my daughter's wedding. Consider this to be a personal invitation."

The Earl glanced over at Well'ngone, who shrugged. This time Well'ngone was truthfully bewildered.

"We usually don't attend social events at the Great Synagogue, Squire," said the Earl. "But since you are Simon's employer, I suppose we could make an exception this once."

"That's right," Well'ngone added. "We can be there in an official capacity. We'll make sure that none of the guests pinch the silver."

✦ ✦ ✦

AND SO MISS HANNAH LYON and Mr. David Goldsmith were married at the Great Synagogue of London, to the immense joy of their families and the great happiness of their community. The courtyard of the Great Synagogue was quite crowded with guests, including Mr. Melamed and Mr. Baer — who were given special honors for their part in making the happy event possible — and Simon and Mr. Warburg and all the employees of Mr. Lyon's shop. And if some of the guests who were gathered around the wedding canopy nervously placed their hands over their pockets when they saw that the Earl of Gravel Lane and General Well'ngone and his men were amongst the company, they had nothing to fear. For on this occasion, all were joined alike in friendship and good will.

If there was one sad note, it was that a suitable young lady has still not been found for Mr. Jacob

Oppenheim, who was also present at the wedding ceremony. Therefore, if anyone should know of a young lady with a good heart and a cheerful disposition, the Narrator requests that a letter, with details, be sent immediately to Mrs. Miriam Baer at Baer's Coffee House, Sweeting's Alley, London, England.

And so with thanks to the Holy One, Blessed Be His Holy Name, for the many kindnesses He has bestowed upon my family, this *megillah* is concluded. And it is concluded just as a proper *megillah* should end — with gladness, song, rejoicing, and exuberance.

End

About the Author

Libi Astaire is an author and freelance journalist who lives in Jerusalem.

She is a frequent contributor to *Mishpacha* magazine, an international Jewish weekly magazine, where she writes about Jewish history and art. Her articles on Jewish spirituality and retellings of traditional Chassidic stories can be found on her own website, Decoupage for the Soul, as well as on Breslev.co.il, a website inspired by the teachings of the Chassidic master Rabbi Nachman of Breslov.

Ms. Astaire grew up in Prairie Village, Kansas. She is a graduate of the University of Michigan,

Ann Arbor, where she received a degree in Theater, English Literature, and European History. She also received an MBA in Marketing and International Business from New York University's Stern School of Business.

In addition to her formal academic studies, she spent a year in London studying theater with instructors from the Royal Academy of Dramatic Arts. While living in New York City, she studied poetry at the New School for Social Research, which awarded her their Pen and Brush Award for poetry in 1979.

Ms. Astaire is also the creator of a popular Israeli detective series for children, which was released on DVD. Her novel about modern-day descendents of Jewish Marranos in Catalonia, Spain, is scheduled to be released in the fall of 2009.

**Watch out for the next
Ezra Melamed Mystery!**

the
Ruby Spy
Ring

By LIBI ASTAIRE

After basking in the excitement and fanfare
of her daughter's recent nuptials, Mrs. Lyon
is at quite a loss how to keep her restless
daughter Rebecca occupied. She is therefore
very grateful when Mrs. Judith Franks, the
mother of Rebecca's friend Harriet, invites

Rebecca for a short visit to their townhouse in Mayfair.

At an art gallery a few days later, Mrs. Franks faints suddenly. Although she recovers quickly, Rebecca notices that the painting that frightened Mrs. Franks is signed by someone named Rembrandt, and it depicts a wedding scene of a young groom standing under a *chuppah*, putting a ruby ring on his bride's finger.

❖ ❖ ❖

A few days later, Mr. Solomon Franks is in his upscale tailor's establishment, measuring a few young men for their uniforms. The shop is quite busy, but once it has cleared out, Mr. Franks discovers a sealed letter on the floor.

To their shock, later that evening, officers of the Crown arrive and inform Mr. Franks that he is under arrest. The charge: Passing military secrets. The evidence: a coded message they have found in his tailor's shop.

❖ ❖ ❖

Shaken and horrified, Mrs. Franks recalls that Mr. Ezra Melamed, the well-known widower and wealthy Jewish businessman from the class of the "gentleman scholar," was of invaluable service to the Lyon family, who only a few months before were on the verge of total financial and social ruin.

No sooner is a messenger dispatched than Mr. Melamed is on the case. Mrs. Franks explains the charges being brought against her husband and then tells him about the painting she saw in the gallery.

Concerned for the future of the Franks family, Mr. Melamed turns to his son-in-law's revered Chassidic Rebbe for assistance in solving the mystery.

Does the painting have something to do with the charges being brought against Mr. Franks? Or is the whole thing a ruse to detract attention from the real spy, who is still passing on important military secrets?

Once again the stakes are high and the clues are few and far between in this new mystery for Mr. Ezra Melamed!